Piranha Picnic

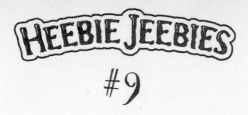

#9

Piranha Picnic

Rod Randall
Created by Paul Buchanan and Rod Randall

BROADMAN
& HOLMAN
PUBLISHERS

Nashville, Tennessee

0–8054–2332–X

Published by Broadman & Holman Publishers,
Nashville, Tennessee

Dewey Decimal Classification: Fiction
Subject Heading: CHRISTIAN LIFE—JUVENILE FICTION
Library of Congress Card Catalog Number: 00–058609

Unless otherwise stated all Scripture citation is from the NIV, the Holy Bible, New International Version, copyright © 1973, 1978, 1984 by International Bible Society.

Library of Congress Cataloging-in-Publication Data
Randall, Rod, 1962–
    Piranha picnic / Rod Randall ; created by Paul Buchanan and Rod Randall.
        p.   cm.—(Heebie Jeebies series ; v. 9)
    Summary: Thirteen-year-old Nick calls upon God when he investigates a possible infestation of his neighborhood river by deadly, flesh-eating piranha.
    ISBN 0–8054–2332–X (pb)
    [1. Piranha—Fiction. 2. Christian life—Fiction. 3. Horror stories.] I. Buchanan, Paul, 1959– II. Title. III. Series.
    PZ7.R15825 Pi 2001
    [Fic]—dc21
                                                           00–058609
                                                           CIP

1 2 3 4 5   05 04 03 02 01

DEDICATION

For Randy

Other books in the Heebie Jeebies series

Chapter 1

We couldn't have picked a worse day for a picnic.

The grass felt like a green sponge from all the rain. My dad had to spread a blue tarp beneath the quilt to keep us from getting soaked. He wanted my mom to be comfortable on our last day together. She had an opportunity she couldn't pass up. Tomorrow she'd be gone.

We were at the riverpark not far from our house. A dreary sky kept us company, along with a blue heron wading near the bank. After missing a fish, the bird let out a deep croak and flapped its giant wings.

So much for the heron.

We were supposed to be enjoying some family time before my mom left us. Normally, we weren't what you would call a real talkative family.

Today we were mute.

I sat cross-legged on the patchwork quilt. A giant beef rib waited for my teeth. The paper plate soaked up the red juice. So did the chips, now soggy. I wasn't hungry, which for me was unheard of. I'm thirteen, have a wiry build, and weigh 140 pounds. But don't be misled; I eat like a horse.

"I still can't believe the river," my dad observed. "I've never seen it this high."

My older sister, Sandy, looked up from her novel. "It's scary." A pink ribbon secured her brown hair in a ponytail. She was sixteen and always reading. Teachers loved her.

I tossed a twig into the chocolate current and watched it drift south. "No, it's not."

The Red River bordered the north side of our town, not in a straight line, but an *S* pattern. Normally it meandered along kind of slow and peaceful. But with all the rain, it had picked up speed . . . and space. Until now, I'd never seen the river as a threat. The southern sun warmed the shallow water for a good seven months a year, making it the perfect place to swim or fish or drift on a raft.

Until now.

"You're sure quiet," my mom said to me.

I grabbed my fishing pole and stood up.

2

"What's to say?" I didn't want to be mean, I just didn't have anything to talk about.

"Nick, don't be that way," my mom called after me.

I waded knee-deep into the river. The water smelled like strong tea and felt almost as warm. A giant willow tree—usually on dry ground—split the current. A thick limb that reached over the water had my name on it. I climbed up and straddled the limb. My lure resembled a silver minnow. I gave it a cast and reeled it in, hoping for a lunker. The disciples had gone fishing when Jesus left them. My parents couldn't blame me for this.

"Nick, you should eat," my mom said.

"Let him starve!" my sister yelled in my direction.

Mom walked to the water's edge carrying the paper plate with the beef rib and chips. I pretended not to notice her.

"Nick, come and get this," she said. She stood on the bank, afraid to venture into the water. The horror of nearly drowning as a little girl still haunted her. She held out the plate.

I stayed put and focused on my next cast. I landed the silver lure fifty feet out, let it drift, then reeled in. The sound of movement against the current caught my attention. I turned to see my mom sloshing through the water. It rose to her shins, then her knees. She kept coming and put the plate on the limb in front of me.

"This was long overdue," she said.

I forced myself to be happy for her. "Way to go, Mom. But I'm still not hungry."

"Nick, you're always hungry." She nudged my side. "Come on. Eat."

I continued to reel the lure through the leaf-stained water. "In a minute. A few more casts."

My mom asked me if I wanted to talk. I shook my head and wouldn't look at her until she sloshed away.

My dad greeted her on the bank with a hug and encouraging words.

My sister joined them. "I'm proud of you, Mom."

They lingered for a moment, then returned to the quilt.

I was still watching them when the fish struck. I couldn't believe it. The minnow lure was so close I had practically lifted it from the water to cast again. I yanked the pole to set the hook. The line sliced across the current. The fish had to be a lunker. It bolted upstream, then circled back. The fight was on. I pictured a ten-pound bass with fierce eyes and a powerful tail. A trophy! Maybe things weren't so bad after all.

Without a net, there was only one way to land it—wade to the bank and drag the giant ashore. I balanced carefully and brought one leg over the limb.

Plunk!

Bummer. I knocked the plate into the water. The rib sank. The plate and chips floated downstream. Oh, well. This was a once-in-a-lifetime fish. I glanced at the water, ready to slide from the limb. I yanked on the pole and gave the reel a few turns. Too easy. The tension was gone.

"No," I moaned. I turned the handle. No resistance. The line went slack. The lunker had thrown the hook. I reeled in, praying the tension would return. It didn't.

No trophy. No fish. I lifted the lure from the water, determined to cast again. Then I saw the damage. Whatever I had hooked had chomped the lure in two.

A swirling beneath me caught my attention. I peered into the water. A fin broke the surface. Then another. A tail splashed. Greenish-brown. The water churned, boiled. Tails. Fins.

Then it stopped. The water flowed like before. No fish. Just ripples. I bent forward and searched the water. I saw something. Long, smooth. What was it? I remembered the rib. But it was covered with sauce and meat when it fell in. I got on my stomach and hugged the limb. I lowered my face to the surface. It sure looked like the rib bone.

But no bass or bluegill could have devoured it that quickly. A catfish would have picked the whole thing up and swam off. I went down the list of fish. Carp. Gar. Suckers. None of those could have cleaned the bone that fast.

I stared into the water. Maybe it wasn't the rib after all. Maybe it was just a smooth stick. Or a pipe. I started to reach for it, but couldn't. I used my fishing pole instead. I pushed the tip under the white whatever-it-was and lifted. It came to the surface, then started to fall. I grabbed it just in time. The rib. Clean. White. Not a shred of meat on it.

Something sharp had scraped it clean.

I thought of the minnow lure with its steel shank snapped in two. A meaty rib scraped to the bone. I stared at the dark water, the water I would have to wade through in bare feet to get to shore. My mom leaving us made me sad. But this was different.

This was scary.

Chapter 2

I eyed the distance—ten feet of river between me and the bank. I would need two steps, one with each foot. "Move fast," I coached myself. "Right foot. Left foot. That was easy."

I brought my feet to the limb and stood up. I balanced with my fishing pole in one hand and the rib in the other. I clenched them like weapons; if only they were.

My dad took up my mom's hand and whispered something in her ear, oblivious to the danger beneath me. I didn't blame him. Let him savor the moment with her. I wasn't about to draw attention to myself. Besides, what would I say? Better to show them the bone and let them decide for themselves.

I released a long slow breath. The next one I held.

Now! I squatted and sprung, expecting to fly through the air.

Sure.

My feet slipped off the limb like it was a greased log.

Splash!

I landed belly first in the water. So much for two steps. Try one flop.

I flailed at the water, unwilling to release the pole and rib. "Argh!"

I pictured razor-sharp teeth on the attack. Torn skin. Blood clouding the water. I gasped and fought for the shore. I stood and slipped. I clawed at the mud and grass. I crawled and kicked. I coughed. The fish. The teeth. The blood.

I lunged for the shore.

Made it! I rolled on my back. My chest rose and filled with a deep breath of air. I closed my eyes and thanked God for delivering me. Then I heard feet squishing over the soft lawn. Pretty soon my family was standing over me, all smiles. Without saying a word, they burst into applause.

"Bravo!" my sister cheered.

"I give him a nine-point-three," Dad added. "Your flying flop had 'Funniest Home Videos' written all over it."

Mom nodded. "It was inspired."

"Knock it off," I said. "I was practically—"

"Is everything all right?" a concerned voice shouted.

My family turned.

I sat up.

A teenage guy materialized from a cluster of bushes upriver. "Is everything OK?"

"I don't know," my sister said with a smirk. "The water's deep here—practically *two* feet. My baby brother almost drowned."

Silence followed.

Laughter followed that. Lots of it.

Even the guy smiled with relief. He had short dark hair and strong arms. He looked like he could swim a mile upriver just for fun. I doubted he was old enough for the university, but I'd never seen him in town before.

"I'm sorry, Nick," my mom said, covering her smile. "What were you saying?"

"Something's out there, that's what." I explained what happened with the minnow lure and rib. My family looked at me like I was nuts. My sister bit the inside of her cheeks to keep from laughing. I waved the bone as proof. "Look at the teeth marks."

"Those are your teeth marks, cheesehead," my sister told me.

The guy stepped back and kept going. "Well, as long as everyone's OK."

"Thanks. We're fine," my dad told him.

The guy turned and walked for the park exit. He glanced back on the way.

My sister, whose eyes hadn't left him, smiled. "Bye."

"Bye," he said with a wave, then disappeared through the trees.

My sister made big eyes at my mom. "He's cute."

"You don't know him?" my mom asked.

My sister sighed. "I wish."

"Great," I muttered. "I was practically killed out there, and all you care about is *cute*." Starting over again, I tried to convince my family that maybe, just maybe, the recent storms had brought something dangerous to the Red River. Something deadly.

My mom smoothed my bushy brown hair away from my forehead. "Don't worry, Nick. Everything's going to be all right."

I could tell we were talking about two different things. And they both scared me.

My mom's eyes embraced us, and wouldn't let go, as if this was the last time we'd be together as a family.

That night I sat on my bed and looked through one of my dad's books, *A Field Guide to North*

American Fishes. I was trying to come up with an explanation for what happened earlier in the day. My best theory was a school of baby gar. I knew they went nuts for meat. Why not a rib? Meat's meat. It made sense. Maybe the sauce drove them into a frenzy. My mom's recipe had done that to me a few times.

I flipped through the glossy pages, still not satisfied.

My mom and dad were in their bedroom. Mom was packing while Dad quizzed her.

"How much cash are you taking?" he wanted to know. Then it was on to where she'd stay and when she'd call. "We'll miss you," he kept saying. Then he'd add, "*I'll* miss you."

My mom didn't respond. She acted like she was going to the ball. She kept asking for my dad's opinion on dresses. He always said the same thing. "Looks great. You should wear it."

The consulting job was too good an opportunity for my mom to pass up. It was supposed to be for a month unless they offered her a permanent position. I tried not to think about that.

"Oh, no!" my mom hollered. "I didn't!"

"What?" my dad asked.

My mom explained that her watch was at the park. She left it on the quilt when she brought me the rib.

My dad called my name a few minutes later. I knew why. I dragged myself into their bedroom. Sure enough, my dad wanted me to jog to the park and look for my mom's watch.

My sister came in. "Don't do it, Nick!" She dropped to her knees in mock horror. "You saw what happened to that rib. What if *you* fall in the river? What if you're next?"

"Knock it off," I said.

"Please," my mom added. She put her hands on my sister's shoulders and tried to guide her out of the room.

Sandy spun around and faced me with her arms crossed. "Go ahead and ask. I know you're thinking it."

"What?"

"You want me to go, don't you?"

My dad raised an eyebrow. "You're volunteering to help your brother? *Volunteering?*"

Sandy pressed her lips together to hold back a smile. "Sure."

My mom forgot about her packing. "It wouldn't have anything to do with that young man we saw there earlier today?"

"Who? *Him?*" My sister dropped her chin, like that was the most ridiculous thing she'd ever heard.

That proved my mom was right. "Nick can go alone," Mom said. "He'll be fine."

Apparently, my mom was as suspicious of that guy as I was, not because he wanted to help me, but because of where he came from, the Thorn plantation. It was off limits to the public. No one had lived there for years. It was overgrown, rotting away, and as rumors had it, haunted. Vagrants and vandals went there, but no one else. It also bothered me that the guy didn't give his name, or stay around long enough to find out ours.

I went to the kitchen and pulled a flashlight from a drawer. I pushed the *on* button. No light. The batteries were dead.

Bad sign.

Chapter 3

Our picnic spot was in a secluded section near the park's boundary. Cypress and dogwood trees blocked out the sky. I moved along the river, doing my best to keep out of it. That was a chore. It had rained steadily for the last two hours. The river had come up even more and filled the low-lying areas of the park. At least I had just been here. I knew exactly where to—

Splash!

Step.

My foot sank up to my ankle. Water poured into my tennis shoe, turning it into a canvas bucket. Each step felt like I was wading. My right foot weighed twice as much as my left. Squish. Step. Squish. Step. I limped along, feeling picked on. "Why me, Lord?" I muttered. I tried to stay on higher ground, but that wasn't easy.

Water had claimed most of the park. Before long, every blade of grass would be seaweed. The town would follow. I thought about the fish that tore the rib to shreds. If our homes went under, what would happen to us?

The humid air stuck to my skin, too hot for October. Summer had been even worse—blistering. The river flowed heavy and rough. One tropical storm had followed another.

I kept going. Squish. Step.

Stop.

Water covered the grass in front of me. Going around it would mean climbing through a dense section of bushes and trees. Not an option. I paced back and forth looking for the best place to cross. From what I could tell, the water was only six inches deep and twenty feet across. No big deal. What could possibly be waiting for me in six inches of water?

I thought of the fins I'd seen. The feeding frenzy. That made me long for dry ground. Or stilts.

I stepped back to get a running start. Sponge shoe number two coming up.

One. Two. Thr—

I held my count. Something thrashed in the river right behind me. *Plunk! Swish!*

I snapped my head around. The thrashing increased. But the darkness and trees worked against me. I couldn't see what it was. I moved closer, holding my breath. Suddenly, the thrashing stopped.

I waited, not sure what to do. Then I decided. I had to cross the flooded section, find my mom's watch, and get home alive.

I started my count again. "One. Two. Three!" I sprang into the water and kept moving. The thrashing started again. It moved along the edge of the river—after me. Water splashed and boiled. I jumped to the end of the flooded section, to higher ground. The thrashing moved in behind me, to the water I had just crossed. I glanced back. A dark figure followed.

"What do you want?" I shouted, while putting distance between us.

It reached the middle of the flooded section, then fell forward. Water erupted around it. Arms reached for me.

"Nick! Help me!" the garbled voice begged. "Ahhh!"

I stopped and doubled back. I had to help. "Nick!" the voice wailed. More thrashing. Arms flailing.

I recognized the voice. A friend from my church. Morris.

He dropped to his knees and beat the frothing water with his fist. "Get away from me!"

I rushed back to the flooded section. My shoes smacked the water. I expected the worst. Jaws ripping at my ankles. Teeth shredding my skin. Fins. Scales. Blood. I grabbed Morris around the chest. I heaved and hauled, bracing myself for the attack, certain I would be next. But I had to help him, to get him out alive or die trying. I stumbled ahead, straining.

"Argh!" Morris wailed.

"Hang on!" I told him. Another step. Then another. We stumbled from the water. I laid Morris down and checked his ankles, expecting to find bloody stumps.

I didn't.

His tennis shoes were fine. Brand new. His ankles were pink, like a baby's.

I looked at his face, beginning to catch on.

He beamed at me. "Greater love has no man than this, that he lay down his life for his friends."

I practically grabbed his ankles and dragged him back in. "Morris, what are you doing here?"

"When I went to your house, you weren't there. Sandy filled me in."

"Obviously," I grumbled. "Did she tell you I have proof?" I gave Morris my side of what happened on the picnic. I promised to show him the lure and rib bone when we got home.

Morris lived a few streets over from us. Normally, he wasn't much of a practical joker. He was too sensitive—about everything. He didn't eat meat because he couldn't stand the thought of killing something. He was friendly enough, just different. We used to hang out when we both played on the same Little League team. But as we got older we grew apart. He became more and more protective of wildlife. Since I loved fishing, that created a problem.

"You should have seen it, Morris. Two words: feeding frenzy." I slopped from shoe to shoe.

"Weird," Morris muttered. He stuck beside me, but kept his eyes on the river.

"So did my sister mention the mystery dude?" I asked.

"Nope."

I told Morris about the guy who appeared from the bushes near the Thorn plantation. "He came out of nowhere, all freaked out."

"You'd freak out too if you came from the Thorn plantation."

"That wasn't it," I explained. "He acted all worried about me. But *why?* Like I would drown in a foot of water! He knows something. You should have seen the fear in his face when he looked at the river."

Morris turned toward the rising water. "Really?"

"Really," I said, my voice somber.

Morris put a clammy hand on my shoulder and made me stop. His deep eyes held mine. "It's payback time, Mr. Fisherman. Now the fish are coming for you."

"Would you knock it off," I said, twisting away.

"You're making too much of this," Morris said. "We've grown up on this river. We know what's out there. Bass. Catfish. Gar. A few snakes. Nothing like you've described."

"I saw what I saw."

"Lures break all the time," Morris reasoned. "I don't even fish and I know that. And anything can pick a rib clean. It's not like we've found any other bones."

We approached the spot where the quilt had been.

"Is that what I think it is?" I asked.

A short pole had been stuck in the ground. My mom's watch dangled from it.

"Someone's looking out for you," Morris said.

"Yeah, that's pretty coo—" I cut myself off and stopped walking. Morris bumped into me and realized why. I couldn't speak. I couldn't move. Neither could Morris.

The pole was a bone. My mom's watch hung two feet off the ground from a clean white bone.

Chapter 4

I didn't tell my mom about the bone. She would have freaked out. As it was, she had enough on her mind.

The family sat in the living room. Mom went over the chores we would divide in her absence. Dad had the grocery shopping. I had the yard and garbage. Sandy had the cleaning. All three of us would share the meals and do the dishes.

My dad stared at the ceiling and listened to the rain come down. "Nick, if this rain keeps up, you can catch us dinner from your bedroom window."

Normally that would've sounded cool, but not now. When I thought about my lure and the rib, I didn't want fish anywhere near my room. Finding my mom's watch propped up on a bone didn't help. Morris thought it was from a deer, but I wasn't so sure. The question of who put it there also haunted me. It had to be the guy who appeared from the Thorn plantation. He must have snooped around after we left. At least he didn't steal the watch. But why hang it from a bone?

"Nick?" Sandy said.

My mom and dad were leaning forward. My sister's hands were folded. They were ready to pray and I had missed the cue. I bowed with them. My mop of brown hair covered my eyes. I forced myself to think about God and not the fish, or river, or rain.

My dad prayed that my mom would do well in her job and that the Lord would keep her safe. He also prayed for us, that we would get by and learn to appreciate Mom even more while she was gone. He closed with *amen* and we straightened up. Mom wiped tears from her eyes and patted my dad's knee.

"Ready, Sandy?" Dad said. Earlier he had asked her to read a certain verse.

"Yep." She read Philippians 2:14. "Do everything without complaining or arguing."

"Why do you think I picked that one?" my dad asked.

I threw in my two cents. "Because Sandy always complains?"

"Funny," Sandy said. She slugged my arm.

"Thanks for proving my point," my dad said. "If we're not careful we'll get irritated with each other and complain about everything. Instead, we need to think of your mom. She stayed home while you were in grade school; now she's working so we can afford college for both of you. We need to encourage her."

I wanted to make a wisecrack, but I didn't. No more pity party. A few extra chores wouldn't kill me. If only I could say the same about what was in the river.

I woke up to my mom sitting on the edge of my bed. She gave me a hug and kiss, then told me to be good and help my dad. I told her I would and that I'd pray for her. She got up to leave and I rolled over to get another hour of sleep. It was six and school didn't start until eight.

I fluffed my pillow and hid my eyes under the covers. Didn't matter. I couldn't sleep. I listened to the garage door open, then got up and looked out the window. My dad stood in his pajamas in the driveway under an umbrella. He blew my mom a kiss as she drove away. Water splashed under the tires and topped the curb. My dad waved until she was out of sight, oblivious to the water around his slippers.

It must have rained all night. The river would have swallowed another two feet of bank. The giant willow tree would be even deeper, harder to get to. But that's where the mysterious fish were.

And that's where I had to go.

That evening I was doing the dishes from dinner when Morris arrived. Along with the fish in the river, my dad's cooking represented a new threat to my life. His roast had enough salt on it to fill an ocean. The potatoes were raw in the center and hard, the broccoli zapped to oblivion.

"What's that smell?" Morris asked.

"Dinner," I told him. "Don't ask."

At first Morris refused to go back to the river with me. He thought it was a waste of time. But I'd kept after him all day at school.

"Forget about it," he had told me. "There's nothing in that river worth bothering. Let it be."

I told him I couldn't and that I was going with or without him. I told him that if I took someone else they might not be so sympathetic to wildlife. I also argued that if we found something, the newspapers would want to know about it. We'd be famous.

That got to him. "Newspapers, huh? OK, I'm in." He agreed to come over after he finished his homework.

I thought that meant afternoon, not after dinner. "What kept you?"

"My mom," Morris said. "She kept finding stuff for me to do."

"I know how that goes," I said. That made me wonder how my mom was doing. I hoped well—but not so well that she wouldn't miss us. "So what'd you have to do?"

"Um . . . you know. Chores. That sort of thing." Morris acted burdened, like he had more on his shoulders than he wanted to admit.

I didn't push it. "Well, let's get out of here before it gets dark."

Sandy lowered her novel to her lap. "Where are you going?"

"Nowhere special," I said.

Sandy kept bugging me until I told her. She immediately wanted to go.

I objected big time. "We're not looking for some *guy*. We're looking for fish—man-eating fish."

"I thought they ate beef," Morris put in.

"You stay out of this," I told him.

Sandy hurried to her bedroom to get her shoes. "Give me two minutes."

"No. You're not coming, and that's final."

So much for final. When my dad didn't back me up, I backed down. I went to the refrigerator and removed two leftover ribs.

Morris and Sandy watched me with curiosity.

"Bait," I said, putting the ribs in a plastic bag.

Next, I grabbed a fishing net that consisted of a long pole with a hoop at the end. Ten minutes later we arrived at the park. We passed the front gate and sloshed over the lawn. More than an inch of water covered the grass. The sun sank across the river. Dusk settled around us. There wasn't a person in sight. We splashed ahead to our picnic spot. The willow tree was at least twenty feet from the bank, ten more than yesterday. The limb I straddled was submerged. The water bulged over it.

"So much for your fishing spot," Sandy told me.

"Big deal," I said. "I wouldn't go back there if you paid me."

Sandy pinched my cheek. "Ah, is little Nicky afraid of some fishy whishys?"

Morris forced an extra loud laugh to encourage her.

"Laugh if you want. You'll see." I removed a rib from the bag and tore off some meat. I tossed it in the water and watched it sink. I waited for the attack. The fins and tails and boiling surface. The teeth. The jaws.

I kept waiting. I tossed in more meat and waited some more.

Did I say I waited? 'Cause I did.

Finally, I tossed in the bone. More waiting. Nothing.

Morris let out a breath, obviously relieved. "Looks like whatever you saw is gone. Oh, well, we tried. Let's go." He started to leave, expecting I would follow.

I didn't.

Sandy tugged my sleeve with a different idea. "Come on. Let's check out the Thorn plantation. There's nothing here."

"Yes, there is." I walked along the bank and repeated the process with the second rib. Still nothing. Morris held the net, but far from the bank.

"Think about it, Nick," Sandy continued. "If that guy came from the Thorn plantation, don't you think we should warn him to stay away? What if he's there now? We know he's not from around here; he probably doesn't know better."

"I'm sure he'll figure it out," I reasoned. "Besides, just because he was there yesterday doesn't mean he's there now."

Sandy shrugged. "You never know."

I inspected the water. The rib rested a foot below the surface—untouched. I glanced in the direction of the Thorn plantation. I'd only been there once, and that was enough. The place seemed cursed, long since dead and left to rot— like bones.

Then something occurred to me. What if there was a connection between the rib, the bone that held my mom's watch, and the Thorn plantation. "I guess it can't hurt to check."

We moved to the edge of the park. A narrow path near the river's edge led through the jungle of tall bushes and dense growth.

"Is this where that guy came from?" I asked.

"I think so," Sandy said. She marched ahead.

But she didn't get far.

Chapter 5

The long white bone blocked the trail. Sandy jumped back and clung to Morris. I moved past them and grabbed the bone.

"Don't touch it!" Sandy squealed.

"Why not? I did yesterday." I explained to her where we found it the first time.

"Mom's watch was on that thing?" Sandy fumed. "Why didn't you say anything?"

"Isn't it obvious?" I pointed out. "Look at you."

Sandy realized her arms were wrapped around Morris' neck. His face brightened as he gave her a mushy grin.

She let go and stepped away. "I'm fine. It just caught me off guard."

Morris offered his opinion of the bone.

"Deer, huh?" Sandy repeated. She thought that made sense but didn't care one way or the other.

She splashed down the path, determined to prove she wasn't chicken. Morris followed. I brought up the rear, holding the bone like a club. I felt like a caveman. "Me Thor," I grunted. "Mighty hunter."

Sandy pushed aside leaves and hanging moss until the Thorn plantation came into view. "How tragic," she mumbled. "And creepy."

She was right on both counts. The buildings that made up the plantation were spread around a cove in the river. The massive white mansion looked like it would collapse under the next drop of rain. Cracks divided the columns that rose from the front porch to the roof. Gray plywood covered the downstairs windows. Broken glass still clung to the upstairs frames. Green shutters dangled from their hinges. Vines smothered the walls.

The barn had one side missing. Roofs had caved in on a few of the smaller buildings. Weeds owned what was once a Bermuda lawn. The broken driveway resembled stepping stones over a marsh.

"Tragic," Morris repeated.

We moved ahead, slower. The weedy soup gave under our feet. Inky water poured into my shoes and soaked my socks. It got deeper with each step. I slapped a mosquito on my neck.

"Forget it," Morris complained. "There's no one here. Let's go."

I agreed, but Sandy kept going.

"Come on, Sis," I urged. "That guy's not here. Let's go back to the river."

She increased her speed. The water splashed away from her feet.

I raised my voice. "There's no one here, Sandy. Stop!" I had grown up hearing horror stories of the haunted Thorn plantation. Supposedly, one of the heirs died mysteriously. The others squandered the family fortune. Eventually, they left the plantation in ruins, scared off by the girl's ghost, or something like that.

Sandy kept splashing away until she saw it and stopped. "No one here, huh?" She pointed at the boathouse on the northern side of the cove. It was raised on posts and hung out over the water. A deck lined one side. A ramp led from the giant rear doors down into the water. Green moss held the whole thing together. "Then what do you call that?"

"Is that a light?" I asked.

No one said anything. The answer was obvious. It was.

"Looks like we found your guy," I said.

"He's not *my* guy," Sandy told me. "You wanted to come here too." She grabbed Morris by the wrist. "You go knock on the door."

"Me?" Morris asked.

I explained what the guy from yesterday looked like. "If it's him, ask if he put my mom's watch on the bone."

"What if it's not him?" Morris asked. "What if it's someone who doesn't want to be found? I've heard rumors about this place."

I patted his back. "Run to my house. We'll be waiting for you there."

Morris stared at the boathouse, debating.

The low sound made up his mind for him. An eerie moan echoed from the upstairs of the white mansion. We watched the broken windows. More moaning. Heavy feet clomped down the stairs.

"New plan," Sandy announced. "Hide." She took off for the nearest cover—the bushes that lined the bank of the river.

"Not there," I called after her. She had the right idea, just the wrong place.

Morris followed Sandy.

"Wait up," I yelled, chasing them.

The moan got louder and moved toward the door. It would be outside soon. After us.

My shoes sunk into the soft earth. They made a suction sound when I lifted them. I plodded ahead. Sandy turned and slipped. *Splat!* She went down fast. Morris did too. They started to rise, but I slipped and flattened them both. We slid down the wet slope into the river. The deer bone dropped from my hand. Morris dropped the fishing net.

Boom! A door at the plantation slammed shut.

"Go! Hurry!" Sandy shouted. She pushed me up.

We crawled through the bushes, ankle deep in current. I parted the leaves and twigs to get through. Sandy and Morris followed, shoving at my back.

The moaning increased, accompanied by heavy feet on the marshy lawn. Closer. Chasing us.

"Faster!" Morris wailed.

I wove ahead. Branches scraped my face. The river rose to my shins, then knees. I prayed for an opening near the bank, and higher ground. But that would expose us to whoever was after us. We had to stay low, beneath the bushes, in the water.

We heard it back there. Wheezing. Tearing at the thick vegetation.

The bushes thinned. I turned and followed the flow toward the park. We'd find higher ground there, if we made it. I beat the bushes and kept going. Sandy and Morris followed.

I listened for the moan and footsteps. Nothing. I prayed it just wanted us to leave. We were—and fast. I splashed ahead. My jeans weighed ten pounds from the water. I took big steps. Then my shoe came off. I stopped. Morris and Sandy went by me.

"Come on," Sandy said, glancing back.

Morris didn't slow down. He just kept going.

"I lost my shoe. Hang on."

The moans returned. I jabbed my hand into the water. I felt the mud and grass. My arm was all the way under. My face nearly touched the surface.

My fingers felt something smooth and round. The toe of my tennis shoe. I grabbed and lifted.

"Ahhh!" Sandy screamed.

I nearly threw up. It wasn't my tennis shoe.

It was a skull.

Chapter 6

"Yuck!" I hollered. A slimy film covered the bone. I tossed it at Morris like a softball.

"Sick." He treated it like a hot potato and threw it to Sandy.

She didn't come close to touching it. "Gross!" She stepped back and let it drop.

"No," I cried. "That's evidence." I hesitated, not sure if I should go after the skull or my shoe.

Feet tromped through the water behind us. Branches snapped. An angry groan rolled with the current.

Decision time. I went for my shoe. I jabbed my fingers in the soft mud, working from side to side. I bumped something! Another round smooth object. I lifted. My shoe! I forced it on, then made a quick grab for the skull.

"Come on, Nick," Sandy said. "Let's go."

"Forget the bones, Nick," Morris said. His white face studied the river and bushes behind us. "It's getting closer!"

"Hurry up!" Sandy demanded, getting mad. "Let's g—" She stopped herself short. "What was that?"

"What was what?" I asked, still reaching up to my shoulder for the skull.

"Something scratched my ankle," Sandy clamored. "Something sharp!"

I yanked my arm out of the water. "You're sure?"

"Positive."

I stared at the brown water. We had stirred up too much mud. The visibility was zero.

"Ahhh!" Sandy screamed. "It did it again."

The steps behind us beat the water. Clumsy. Loud. Branches snapped.

Sandy took off, but stumbled. The river swirled to her waist. She got up and kept going. Morris and I followed, before the next bones found were ours.

I tried to stay near shore, but the high water and evening gray blurred the boundaries. The jungle of growth didn't help. I pushed branches and vines aside. Sandy and Morris had vanished. I followed their voices and feet. At least I could still hear them . . . at first.

"Wait up," I yelled. I eased my shoes from the mud fearing I'd lose them. I sloshed through the water, listening. "Sandy? Morris?"

They didn't answer.

The moan behind me did. It approached on my right, closer to the bank.

I kept going, determined to reach the park. The leaves and bushes formed a green maze, but at least it wasn't as deep. The water dropped from my thighs to my knees. My heart pounded. My side ached. I weaved through the dense vegetation. Almost there.

Then a hand grabbed my throat.

Before I could scream, another covered my mouth.

I turned in horror.

Morris held me with one hand. Sandy with the other. They pulled me into the center of a dense bush.

"Shh!" Sandy warned.

We held our breaths. We waited.

Water splashed. Branches snapped.

"I think it got ahead of us," Morris whispered. He pointed further up the bank. We listened. Sure enough, something was there.

I clenched my teeth so they wouldn't chatter. "What now?"

Sandy reached out and snapped loose a reed.

Then she broke off the top. It was a foot long and hollow, double the size of a straw.

I knew what she was thinking. "No way." I reminded her that something had just attacked her ankle.

"It was probably just a stick," she told me. "I'm fine. Come on, make a snorkel. We'll drift past him." She drew a breath through the reed to show me how well it worked.

Morris shook his head with conviction. "Forget it. I'd rather face the plantation zombie." He edged further into the bush and lifted himself. "I'm staying up here."

It was nice to have Morris on my side for once.

Sandy stared at the stained water. Our lack of support got to her.

I told them my plan. We'd wait a little longer, then silently stalk whatever was stalking us. Once we saw it, we'd decide what to do. Morris liked my idea. Sandy gave me the nod. We left the safety of the bush. Our ankles and muddy shoes pushed silently through the current. Not a sound. We took our time, finding the gaps in the bushes. Ten feet. Twenty. We eased ahead, as quiet as shadows, our feet sinking in the soft mud. The park finally came into view.

Deserted.

The river swept over the lawn and fingered its way through the foliage. The willow tree held its ground. The half moon offered enough light to make out some picnic benches, parking spaces, and further down, restrooms. But that was all. No people. The plantation ghoul was gone.

I motioned for Sandy and Morris to join me behind a dogwood tree. "It could be waiting to ambush us. As soon as we reach the shore, we sprint."

They nodded.

I started again. Mud gave way to grass. The water dropped to our shins, then ankles. The shore was five feet away. Three feet. One.

We took off! We had sponges for shoes and sopping wet pants, but we hauled. Past the willow tree. Past our picnic spot. We ran on. Past the restroom and barbecue pits. I kept thinking something would lunge from behind a tree. I thought of the skull and deer bone. How many more bones were out there? And why?

We made it to the park entrance. Our house wasn't far—over the bridge, across the highway, to our neighborhood. I started to relax. Then a shout sent a shiver down my spine.

"You!" a deep voice called out. "Come here!"

No chance. It was night, bones littered our wake, and after what we'd heard, stopping was out of the question.

"Keep going," I gasped. My shoes and wet jeans fought against me, but I couldn't give up. Sandy and Morris ran like river rats, covered with silt and slime. We splashed the pavement, striding on. We reached our street. Our house.

We flung open the front door and slammed it behind us. Sandy locked the door, the deadbolt, and even slid the brass chain into the track.

I pressed my back against the door, just to make sure. A brown puddle spread on the white tile beneath me. Sandy and Morris hurried across the living room carpet to the kitchen and started their own puddles. My mom would have killed us for coming inside sopping wet. But the carpet would dry. At least we were home. Safe. I let out a long slow breath.

Then something dense thumped the outside of the door.

Boom! Boom! Boom!

Chapter 7

Morris and Sandy stared at me, waiting for me to react.

I swallowed and waited. I hoped my dad would hear the noise and come from the other room. He didn't.

Sandy spoke up. "See who it is." She pointed at the peephole in the front door.

I turned and held my breath. My imagination took over. I prepared for a Thorn zombie staring back at me. I cringed at Sandy and offered my "are you sure about this?" face.

Boom! Boom! Boom!

My heart thumped in high gear. I brought my eye to the brass circle that encased the glass. I squinted, fearing the worst.

That's not what I found.

It was the guy from the picnic, the teenager. He

looked at his feet, acting innocent and out of place.

I unlocked the door and deadbolt, but left the chain in place.

"Hi, I'm Toby Timber," the guy said. He stretched his neck to get a look behind me. "I work at the park. Is everything all right?"

"Um . . . yeah. Everything's fine," I told him.

He eyed my soaked pants and the puddle beneath my feet.

Before I could say anything, my dad came strolling into the living room. He noticed the water right off. "What's going on here?"

I closed the door. "It's that guy from the picnic. He wants to know if we're OK."

My dad brought his hand to his chin. "I don't blame him. You should see yourselves." He told me to open the door.

"No," Sandy blurted out, raising a hand. "He can't see me like *this!*" She rushed down the hall to her room.

My dad, Morris, and I rolled our eyes in unison. I removed the chain and opened the door.

Toby stood there with his hands in his pockets. His blue T-shirt had the name of the local university across the front.

My dad invited him in. "Watch the puddle. You'll slip."

I joined Morris in the kitchen.

Toby introduced himself again and explained that he saw us running and screaming and wanted to make sure everything was all right.

"Is it?" my dad asked, turning to me and Morris.

I stood there forming a new puddle. "Um . . . yeah. Sure." I kept my answer short on purpose. Toby's repeat appearance under the pretense of *helping* seemed suspicious.

"As long as you're OK," Toby said. "You guys were freaking out. I thought something had to be wrong." He explained that he was a new student at the university and an intern with the Parks and Recreation Department.

My dad voiced what I was thinking. "The university, huh?"

"Yeah, I know I look young," Toby said, taking it in stride. "I graduated from high school a year early. I'm only seventeen. Anyway, with the river at flood stage, you should be careful. The current is stronger. Trees are being uprooted. Basically, the whole ecosystem is a mess."

"Tell me about it," I blurted out. "You should have seen the fi—" I stopped myself short, realizing I had almost spilled the beans.

"Seen what?" Toby asked.

"The . . . um . . . ."

My dad sighed in frustration. "Nick dropped a

rib in the river and supposedly some fish stripped it clean."

"What kind of fish?" Toby asked. He squinted at me, like I knew something he did, but shouldn't.

"Beats me," I said, volunteering nothing.

"Could have been anything," Morris put in. "Gar. Bluegill. Bass."

"I doubt it," Toby said. "Those fish wouldn't account for the bones that have turned up."

"Bones?" my dad repeated. "I thought there was just the rib."

Toby shook his head. "We've found more."

That made me think of the deer bone. "You didn't use one to prop up a watch, did you?"

He told me he didn't, then shifted the attention back to me. Reluctantly, I described the fish in more detail. Greenish backs. Blunt heads. Swirling water. I also told him about the deer bone and skull.

"If I were you, I'd stay away from the river," Toby warned.

"Any idea what's going on?" Dad asked.

"It's probably just the rain," Morris put in. "The fish are all riled up, so they're eating anything in sight."

"Not likely," Toby offered. "Even riled up fish don't rip flesh from bones, at least not the fish in our river."

"They could have come in from another river," Morris said. "Or a flooded pond."

Toby shrugged. "The species would be the same."

"What's your theory, Toby?" my dad asked.

"Well, from what you described, it sounds like . . . nah, forget it." Toby shook his head and opened the front door.

"What?" I asked. "What?"

He kept shaking his head, unwilling to accept his own theory. I could tell he didn't want to say it. We waited, watching him.

"Piranha." Toby's dark eyes met mine. "Piranha."

Chapter 8

Piranha.

I pictured the word and the fish that went with it. Razor-sharp teeth. Muscle and bone wrapped in scales. Killing machines. They attacked in schools and ripped the flesh from anything that crossed their path. Not piranha. Anything but that. I watched Toby, to see what he would say next.

But Morris did the talking. "Piranha? They're from the Amazon. That's in South America."

"I know where the Amazon is," Toby said.

"There's no way," Morris continued. "Piranha in the Red River? No chance."

Toby lifted his hands. "I didn't say there was. I'm just going by the description he gave me."

"Piranha," Morris repeated, shaking his head. He forced a laugh. "Sure."

"What about piranha?" Sandy asked, coming down the hall. Her long brown hair was dark from the water and combed back over her head. She had on white shorts, a green blouse, and make-up.

"Um . . . hi," Toby said, straightening up. All at once, he seemed confounded by his hands. He put them in his front pockets, then pulled them out and crossed his arms. Next he tried his back pockets.

My sister noticed and smiled. "Hi, I'm Sandy."

Toby introduced himself, then placed his right hand on the back of a chair and leaned. Too bad it reclined under his weight. He fell forward, but managed to catch himself before hitting the ground.

Morris cracked up. Normally, I would have too, but all I could think about was piranha. No wonder the rib disappeared so fast. No wonder bones were turning up left and right.

My dad updated Sandy on what we had discussed.

"Piranha would explain the bones," Sandy agreed. "But this is North America, not South America."

"Maybe someone imported them," I suggested. "Like killer bees. They originated in Africa. Now they're everywhere. Why not piranha?"

I looked around, ready for someone to shoot me down. But no one did. The ramifications of a piranha invasion and flooded town kept everyone silent.

The next few days didn't go very well. Stuff that was normally put away began to crowd our living space. Dirty dishes and laundry. Junk mail and newspapers. The house got messier and my dad got grumpier.

To make things worse, the river flooded more land, bringing the piranha closer to home.

Toby started calling my sister after his visit. Sandy would sit diagonally in the recliner and wrap the phone cord around her finger, beaming. My dad had to limit her time or she would talk for hours. She acted like Toby was the cutest, bravest, smartest guy on earth. "He graduated a year early," she would say after hanging up. "A year early."

I withheld my admiration, mainly because I still didn't trust the guy. Supposedly he had told his superiors at the Parks and Recreation Department about the possibility of piranha. But when I went there I didn't see any signs warning people to stay away from the water. I couldn't believe it. A deadly threat and no warning signs. It didn't make sense.

I was also haunted by what happened at the Thorn plantation. Why had someone gone to such great lengths to scare us away? The place was abandoned, falling apart.

And then there was the boathouse. We saw the light. Heard the door slam. Something was going on there, and I had a hunch Toby was involved. Of course he denied it when Sandy asked. He thought it was funny that we were so freaked out. But there was nothing funny about it.

My dad had cautioned me about going back to the park but hadn't forbidden it, mainly because he thought the idea of piranha in the river was impossible. Sandy no longer cared about the river at all. She just wanted to impress Toby. She shifted her reading to cookbooks, with the plan to have him over for dinner.

Morris was the hardest to figure out. On the one hand, he laughed at the thought of piranha in the Red River, but on the other, he flatly refused to go back. That meant I'd have to return alone, and would, just as soon as I did my research.

I checked out some library books, took them home, and started reading. Piranha came in several varieties with hard-to-pronounce scientific names like *Serrasalmus nattereri*. They averaged about fourteen inches long. Their colors included black, gray, olive-green, or a combination of all three. They were aggressive by nature, had stocky torsos, blunt heads, and powerful jaws. One book said that piranha teeth were so sharp and fit together so well that Indians used them for scissors. Scariest of all was how piranha reacted to blood—feeding frenzy. They could strip a cow to a skeleton in minutes.

The more I read, the more my imagination took over. I found myself knee deep in the Red River fighting piranha. I wielded the deer bone like a club. I thumped the piranha and sent them packing. But more came. Ten turned into a hundred. A hundred became a thousand. No problem. I led them to a net attached to the willow tree. I gave Morris the signal and he hoisted them up. Caught. Every one. The river was safe again.

Then the phone rang. The clock said 9 P.M. My mom's call was right on schedule. Dad talked to her first. He was in the living room and was easily overheard. He started with questions. My mom's answers must have been good. "Great," my dad said. "That's wonderful. Wow, I'm impressed."

I wasn't. I was happy for my mom, but feared that if it was going that well, she'd consider extending her stay. My dad talked for a while and gradually changed his tone, especially when he told her how things were going around here. The rain had slowed some in our area, but not up north, so the river continued to rise. That must have really scared my mom, because pretty soon he was telling her it wasn't as bad as it sounded. "We sure miss you," he kept saying over and over again.

Sandy got on the phone next. I moved into the kitchen and took my time getting a glass of punch. I wanted to hear how Sandy would report on our adventure to the Thorn plantation. She didn't. All she could talk about was Toby. Words like "so cute," and "genius," made me want to listen from the bathroom in case I needed to throw up.

"Wait until you hear Toby's last name," Sandy said. "Timber. Toby Timber. Don't you just love it?"

My mom must have covered the phone to laugh, because after a few seconds, Sandy asked, "Mom, are you there?"

After that the conversation picked up again. My mom asked all kinds of questions about Toby. Sandy went on and on. I tuned out. The next thing I knew, Sandy was calling for me. My turn.

"Hi, Nick," Mom said. "How's my great fisherman?"

"Not so good."

"I understand you made another visit to the park and river."

"Yeah. A few days ago."

"You're not going back, I hope."

"I don't know, maybe. Dad said—"

"I think you should stay away from there for a while, at least until the water goes down."

"Mom, I'll be OK," I told her. "Plus, I still need to see what's out there."

"What do you mean, 'what's out there'?"

I cringed, knowing I had said too much.

"Um . . . you know. The weird fish that ate the rib."

"You mean the piranha."

"What?" I gasped. "Who told you?"

"Your dad. And I agree with him, it's pretty far-fetched. But just to play it safe, I think you should stay away from the river."

I started to whine. "Mom, you already said that."

"I know. I'm your mother, remember?"

"Sorry, I forgot. You better come home—fast." I told her how hard it was without her and that dad's cooking almost killed us. "I doubt Sandy will do much better."

"Next weekend," my mom said, reminding me when she would visit. "Two weeks after that I'll be home to stay."

I told her that sounded good, then gave the phone back to my dad. He carried it to the bed-room and closed the door.

I went to Sandy's room to ask her how Mom reacted when she heard about Toby.

"I don't know," Sandy said, looking up from her cookbook. "Like she always does when I tell her about a guy. She wanted to know everything about him."

"Ah ha," I said. "Maybe Mom's as suspicious of him as I am. Women's intuition. Doesn't it bother you that both times something creepy happened at the river Toby showed up?"

"No, not at all." Sandy stood up and pushed me from her room. "What bothers me is having a paranoid little brother."

I twisted around her and jumped for the bed.

She grabbed me again, but my dad came in before she could yank me out. His expression was heavy, burdened.

"What's wrong, Dad?" Sandy asked.

He had us both sit down. "Kids, there's something I need to tell you about your mother."

Chapter 9

My dad spread his hand over his forehead and massaged his temples. "Your mother is really concerned with what's happening to the river."

"I don't blame her," I agreed. Then I realized where this might be going and backpedaled. "Don't worry, Dad. I'll be careful."

"Let me finish, Nick." He cleared some clothes from Sandy's dresser and half-leaned, half-sat. "You both know your mother's afraid of swimming. For her to wade to her knees was a miracle." My dad reminded us that my mom had nearly drowned as a child. "She never told you where it happened, did she?"

"Nope," I said.

My dad pointed out the window. "It happened in the Red River."

"Our river?" I asked. "The one just down the street? I can't believe Mom never told us."

My dad helped us understand my mom's motives. She didn't want us to be paranoid of the Red River because of what happened to her. She still loved watching it, the lazy bends and ripples and birds. "She has worked her whole life to overcome the fear of what happened on that day."

I sat in silence, trying to put the pieces together. "Why tell us now, Dad, with Mom gone?"

"It has to do with the flooded banks . . . and the Thorn plantation."

"I don't get it," Sandy said.

"That's where it happened. Your mother was playing with her brother in the trees that reached out over the cove. The groundskeeper let them, even though he wasn't supposed to. The current was too dangerous. A whirlpool had formed in the cove beside the boathouse. Your mother fell in and couldn't get out. Her brother went for the caretaker. He launched a boat and grabbed your mom just as she went under. She was unconscious when he brought her to shore, but eventually he revived her."

"Then what happened?" I asked.

My dad tilted his head from side to side. "They took her to the hospital. Physically, she was fine, but emotionally, she never got over the feeling of being sucked down while water filled her lungs." My dad stood up. "When she was released from the hospital, the groundskeeper was gone. The Thorn family fired him on the spot and he left town."

"Why? Because he saved Mom's life?" I asked. The story confirmed everything I had ever heard about the Thorn family. "If the groundskeeper had let Mom die, they probably would have given him a raise."

"I doubt it. I didn't bring this up so you would hate the Thorn family. I brought it up so you would understand your mother—and why it's dangerous to be around there. Got it?"

I nodded.

"No trespassing means just that," my dad emphasized. "Stay away from the Thorn plantation."

"Tell that to Toby. He's the one we should keep our eyes on."

"Not again," Sandy moaned.

"And don't forget the piranha. If they're out there, a whirlpool is nothing compared to what they can do. Wait here." I ran and got my books. "See this! Look at those teeth!"

"Nick, what are you driving at?" my dad asked.

"I want to catch them. Whatever it takes. Traps. Nets. Hooks. Anything." I went on and on about my plans.

My dad waited patiently for me to finish, even though he didn't believe piranha had invaded the Red River. "Nick, stay away from the Thorn plantation and be careful. Otherwise, you can catch all the piranha you want." With that he left the room.

Sandy thought I should do the same and shoved me into the hall. "One more thing: don't scare off Toby with your stupid theories. OK?"

"They're not—"

Sandy closed her door before I could finish. I headed for my room but never made it. My dad reminded me that it was my turn to take care of the garbage.

I forced myself not to grumble. I remembered the Bible verse Sandy read the night before my mom left. "Do all things without complaining." My dad normally brought in the garbage cans, but with him covering my mom's chores, I had to cover his.

Water splashed away from my feet on the front walkway. The ditches that lined the street were full. The drainage pipe that ran under our driveway couldn't handle the brown flow. Water spread to the sidewalk and yard. I sloshed through it, thinking about my mom and how horrible it must have been to nearly drown. I actually found myself looking up the street to make sure a whirlpool wasn't waiting for me. It didn't make sense, but I couldn't help it. The idea of my lungs filling with brown river water gave me the heebie jeebies.

I quickly grabbed a trash can and started for the house. It felt half-full, instead of empty. I turned it on its side and let the rainwater drain. I put it beneath the eave of the garage, then went for the next one. This time I drained it before starting for the garage. I was halfway there when I heard something banging around in the bottom of the can.

It wasn't until I was under the floodlight on the garage that I could see what it was. Then I wished I couldn't.

It was white, wet, and round.

A skull.

"Not again!" I gasped. I stepped back from the trash can as if the skull was alive. I squeezed my fingers into fists then relaxed them again, trying to figure out what to do. Why was there a skull in our trash can? What was it from? I took a deep breath, tensed my stomach, and stepped forward for another look.

I leaned over, careful. Timid.

It was still there, face up. The empty sockets stared back at me.

Slowly, I lowered my hand into the trash can. Easy. A little lower. My fingers trembled. Got it.

"GROWL!!!" an animal roared.

"AHHHH!" I dropped the skull and jumped back. I looked around.

A savage roar shook the bushes next to the garage.

I stumbled and fell backward on the lawn.

The bushes shook. Another growl.

Then Morris sprang into view. He raised his hands like claws, doing his best standing grizzly. "Grrr!"

I jumped to my feet, ticked off. I felt like making him eat the skull. "Funny, Morris. Real funny."

"You're a stress case," he said. He tilted his head to check out my soaked back.

"What do you expect?" I shot back. I pointed into the trash can.

Morris reached in and pulled out the skull like it was no big deal. He held it with one hand and rubbed his chin with the other. "To be or not to be, that is the question."

"Knock it off," I said, taking the skull away from him. It was about the size of a baseball, and round like a monkey's. "Nice prank, Morris. Real funny."

Morris held up his hands. "Don't blame me."

"Sure."

"I'm serious."

I looked around, up the street, then down, trying to make sense of it. At first glance I didn't see anything. Then I caught sight of a dark figure standing next to a tree, about three houses down. I held still and did my best ventriloquist. "Psst, Morris," I pointed with my chin.

He turned just as the dark figure disappeared.

Chapter 10

Morris stared down the street. "What?"

"Someone was there," I told him.

"I don't see anyone."

"Go down there. You will."

Morris stood his ground. "No thanks. I believe you. It's probably the guy who lives there."

"Mr. Decker?" I called out. "Is that you?"

I kept my eyes on the tree.

No answer. No movement.

"So much for the guy who lives there." I considered my options and decided on the safest: my dad. Morris agreed to watch the tree while I got him. My dad came out with a flashlight and turned over the skull a few times. Next, he headed to the tree down the street. Morris and I walked beside him.

"Hello?" he offered.

No answer.

He motioned for us to stand back. Then he sprang around the tree.

There was a thud, followed by nothing.

Morris looked at me.

I shook my head.

Silence.

"Dad?" I said. "Are you all right?" I eased to the tree. Step-by-step. "Dad, are you—"

"Gotcha!"

I gasped, then I realized it was my dad. "You're as bad as Morris."

"Sorry, Nick. I couldn't resist." My dad put his arm on my shoulder and walked me around the tree. "There's no one here."

I grabbed the flashlight and inspected the ground. "What about those?"

Large shoes had left two kinds of footprints in the soft mud.

We looked at my dad's shoes. His matched one set. The other looked like a waffle iron.

"Weird," my dad admitted. He searched the street some more but didn't find a thing. "Someone else was here, all right."

We headed back to our house and took a closer look at the skull. My dad guessed it was from a rabbit. The fact that it was in our trash can bothered him. "You're sure you saw someone?"

I nodded, gravely. I didn't know what was going on, but I had a gut feeling it had something to do with piranha and the haunted Thorn plantation.

Two days later no more clues had turned up, so I decided to shift my attention to Toby. He was coming for dinner. Sandy had read about a gourmet meal and wanted to fix it for Toby. The word *gourmet* made my stomach queasy. I imagined eating something like stuffed snails or poached spinach medley.

I consoled myself with the fact that with Toby in our house, I could lure him into my trap. I didn't want Sandy to know about it, so I quietly slipped from the dining area to the back patio. It took just a few minutes to set up the dart board. From there, I went to my room to have another look at the skull. According to my biology teacher, it was from a large rabbit. He guessed the rains had washed it into the ditch and someone dropped it in our garbage can. I didn't buy it. Something was going on. And for some strange reason it kept revolving around me.

When the doorbell rang, I emerged from my room. A cloud of smoke waited for me. I had to crawl on my belly to keep from choking. I soon found out that Sandy had decided on stuffed mushrooms, cauliflower, and blackened sea bass. It was the *blackened* part that got the best of her.

"Hit the deck!" I shouted at my dad.

He hurdled me en route to the smoke alarm, but didn't get there in time. The siren wailed.

I made it to the front door and pulled it open. "Hey, Toby. Welcome to Sandy's Smokehouse."

"Looks like it," he said, squinting. He stepped past me and started coughing right away.

Once my dad quieted the smoke alarm, he opened the windows and doors.

"Dinner time," Sandy sang, like everything was perfectly normal. She brought the food to the table while the rest of us sat down. The smell of rotten vegetables and burnt fish filled the dining room. I breathed only when necessary and then through my mouth.

Once everything was on the table, my dad said grace—with noticeable caution.

"Looks great," Toby said, smiling at my sister.

I looked at him like he was nuts. But he didn't notice me. His sights were set on Sandy. With the two of them locked in some sort of crush trance, I employed every get-through-the-meal trick I knew. I took tiny portions, heaped on the ketchup, and spit bites into my napkin. When I had to swallow, I bypassed my taste buds by shoving my fork to the back of my mouth.

My dad did the same thing.

But not Toby. He savored each bite like a love-sick food critic. "This is *so* good," he announced. "Mmm . . . mmm."

"Have more," Sandy cooed.

He did. Seriously. Evidently, Toby liked my sister even more than I thought.

Half-begging, half-praying, I whispered, "Mom, please come home."

"What was that?" Sandy asked.

"Oh, nothing," I said. To change the subject I asked Toby if any piranha had been found in the river.

A heavy weight filled his eyes. Lines creased his forehead. "You didn't hear it from me, but we're on the verge of a national emergency. Forget about a *few* piranha. We're talking thousands of piranha. And with the river on the rise, it won't be long until the entire town is eaten alive."

I stopped midchew and slammed my hand on the table. "I knew it! Seeeee? You guys didn't believe me. But it's true."

My dad caught Sandy's eyes, then Toby's. They joined in a chorus of laughter. Lots of it.

"Thousands of piranha?" my dad repeated. He took a big bite of blackened bass. "That's a lot of fish. Hope they're good eating."

"Oooo, I'm so scared," Sandy cried, wiggling her hands in the air.

"Laugh all you want," I fumed. "But we never used to find bones in the river—not until last Sunday . . . when we met Toby."

A shoe kicked me under the table. Sandy cleared her throat and rebuked me with her eyebrows. I backed off. Without Toby's cooperation, my plan wouldn't work.

Once we finished dinner, I led Toby out back for a game of darts. Sandy and my dad stayed in the kitchen cleaning up.

Toby threw first, then I went. My first two darts hit the board, but the third missed entirely.

I hustled to find it in the wet grass beyond the patio. "Did you see where it went?"

Toby joined me and found it. "Here you go."

As soon as he stepped on the dry concrete I knew my trap had worked. His wet shoes left a print of the same pattern we had seen that night under the tree. The waffle grid. Toby could joke all he wanted about thousands of piranha. I didn't care. He was up to something. He had been to our house and left the skull. If I didn't trust him before, I really didn't trust him now.

Time for phase two. When Sandy finished the dishes, we concluded our game and Toby joined her in the living room. I headed for the den to call

Morris. We had to move fast. I opened the church directory, found his number, and dialed. Busy. I waited and dialed again. Still busy. Good thing he only lived four blocks away. I could run over and get him before Toby left.

When I asked Dad about going to see Morris, he hedged. "Can't it wait?"

I shook my head. My dad reluctantly let me go. I threw on my raincoat and went through the garage so Sandy and Toby wouldn't notice me leaving.

Then I ran. Make that sprinted. It was a school night; Toby wouldn't be allowed to stay at our house long. Morris and I didn't have much time.

Chapter 11

I pushed the lit doorbell button. Muffled chimes filled the house. The porch light came on and Morris's mom opened the door. She had on gray sweats and her hair was tied back. A workout video was playing on the TV.

I asked for Morris.

"He's out back," she said, taking note of my wet shoes. "The side gate's open."

I hurried past the garage door and pushed through the wooden gate. Once it closed behind me, I couldn't see a thing. The clouds blocked out the moon and stars. The gate and house and trees blocked out the porch light. My eyes had adjusted on the way over, but not enough.

I stayed next to the garage wall, feeling my way. Something wet caught my face. I squirmed and pulled it away. It was a cloth of some kind.

"Morris?"

He didn't answer.

"Morris?"

I kept going. The garage ended. I touched the dark air and moved ahead. I squashed through soft grass. "Morris? Are you back here?"

I held my hands in front of me, stepping slowly. I called his name again.

"Over here," he said.

"Finally." I picked up speed. Time was our enemy.

"Don't come any further," Morris warned.

"Why? What's the—"

Splash! My foot dropped into a hole. I fell back to keep my body from following it.

"I told you to stop," Morris complained, turning on a flashlight. "What's the rush?"

I had stepped into a large pond that filled the majority of his backyard. Morris was kneeling on the grass with a dead fish in front of him. It looked like a giant goldfish.

"What's going on?" I asked.

"I'm just praying. We lost another one."

I didn't know what to say. Apparently the fish meant a lot to Morris. Until now I didn't know he had a pond, let alone pet fish.

Morris picked up the fish and headed for a shed nearby. I followed, filling him in on the way.

He grabbed a shovel and walked to the back of the property. He dug a hole and carefully lowered the dead fish to the bottom.

"You should plant a corn seed with that," I said, trying to lighten the mood.

Morris failed to appreciate my sense of humor.

I backpedaled. "Sorry, dude. I didn't know you were so into fish."

"There's a lot about me you don't know."

I wondered what he was getting at, but didn't pursue it. All I could think about was Toby and the matching footprints. "We've got to hurry. Are you in?"

Morris returned the shovel to the shed. "Sure. I'm in." He told his mom we were going for a run. He wasn't kidding. We sprinted down the street, turned right, then sprinted some more. We rounded the corner to my street just as my sister escorted Toby to his Jeep.

I stopped, but my feet didn't. They flew into the air. I landed with a splat. Morris tumbled over me, driving my elbow into the cement. I could feel it bleeding but didn't care. We scrambled behind a tree, the same tree Toby had hid behind after leaving the skull. The blood from my scrape trickled to the end of my elbow, then dripped into a mud puddle at my feet.

"Now what?" Morris asked.

I peeked around the trunk. Toby said goodbye to Sandy, then got in his truck and started the engine. She watched him back into the street.

"Get down," I ordered. We hunkered close to the tree. Toby cruised by but didn't look in our direction. I checked on Sandy. She had gone inside. Perfect. We waited for Toby to turn the corner. "Let's go!"

Dogs barked in our wake as we took off after Toby. We passed houses in a blur, then cut through a field. Toby had to drive through several streets to leave the neighborhood. We could almost beat him by cutting through open lots and jumping fences.

Morris matched my stride. We splashed through puddles, crossed yards, and ducked branches. We soaked up water with each step. Our pants grew heavier, shoes too, but we kept going.

We hopped the fence just as Toby drove from the neighborhood. He stopped at Frontage Road to let some cars pass. If he turned right, there was nothing we could do; Frontage Road would eventually lead him to the university. But if he went straight, we would follow. The road crossed the river. The park was on the other side, and beyond that, the Thorn plantation. Nothing more.

Morris sounded like he would hyperventilate. I took deep breaths and bent forward with my hands on my waist. I hoped the cars would keep coming.

They didn't.

Toby's brake lights dimmed. He took off. Straight. He crossed the river.

"Come on," I said. We continued our chase, staying to the side of the road in case Toby checked his rearview mirror. We followed him over the bridge. The dark river rolled beneath us, lapping at the shore. We hid while Toby unlocked the pole that blocked the park access.

"What'd I tell you?" I said.

Morris nodded. "Bingo."

After driving past the entrance, Toby locked the pole behind him. He returned to his Jeep and took off into the trees. We did too. We ran past the entrance and searched for taillights. More running. Searching. His Jeep was gone. We made our way through the park. The road ended at a locked gate. On the other side was the Thorn plantation.

"I knew it," I said.

"Knew what?" Morris questioned. "We still don't know what Toby's up to."

"Not yet," I said. "But we're going to find out."

"We should ask Sandy," Morris suggested.

"Don't say a word to her. She'd tell Toby, and he'd never let us follow him again." I checked my elbow. It dripped red.

Suddenly the Jeep's engine rumbled toward us. We saw headlights. In no time they were upon us. One side of the road offered flat grass with no cover. The other side had the river. "Come on," I said. I grabbed Morris's arm. We rushed down the bank into the river. We ducked our heads behind some reeds. The warm current flowed waist deep. The piranha came to mind. We weren't far from where I had dropped the rib.

Toby stopped on the plantation side of the gate and unlocked it. After driving his Jeep through, he jumped out and locked the gate again.

That's when I noticed he wasn't alone.

My heart jumped. My eyes grew.

Toby had picked up a passenger. An old man with a sour face. He had white hair and wrinkled skin, bulky chest and shoulders. He filled the bucket seat and then some. I thought of the moan and thundering steps that chased us from the Thorn plantation.

I held my breath until they drove away. "Morris, did you—"

"Look out!" he warned. He grabbed my arm and yanked it out of the water.

Chapter 12

I scrambled onto the bank. "What? What?"

"Piranha!" Morris gasped. He crawled beside me. "They attack when there's blood."

We watched the water.

Morris pointed at the dark surface. "See that?"

I studied each ripple. "Nope. But I believe you." I scooted higher on the bank and kept my eyes on the water. I thought I saw a fin, but couldn't tell. "Let's get out of here."

We stood and sloshed from the river. We made our way toward the park entrance, using trees to keep out of sight. I asked Morris if he was thinking the same thing I was about the old man.

"It could have been him," Morris admitted. "But why would he want to scare us off?"

Toby repeated his unlocking/locking routine at the park entrance. The old man never got out of the Jeep. They crossed the bridge, then turned on Frontage Road in the direction of the university.

"This is getting weirder all the time." I sat down and removed my shoes. Water poured out.

Morris copied me. "Maybe we shouldn't have followed Toby. What did it accomplish?"

"Are you crazy? Now we know he's connected to the Thorn plantation. We also know he's not in on it alone."

"In on what?" Morris fumed. He didn't expect an answer, and I didn't have one. Since yanking my arm out of the water, he had avoided my eyes. He looked down mostly, like he couldn't bear to watch what might happen next.

I gave him a pat on the back to cheer him up. "Don't give up, Morris. We'll figure this out. God will help us."

We paused on top of the bridge and looked down at the river. It rolled by. I imagined what was happening beneath the brown surface. A school of deadly piranha darting about, snapping their razor-sharp teeth at whatever flesh they could find.

Morris sloshed toward home. He didn't seem to care if I caught up with him or not. I did anyway and asked him what was wrong.

He said, "Nothing," but his features said otherwise. He stuck his hands in his wet pockets. His shoulders slumped. His face hung parallel to the sidewalk.

"Seriously," I said. "What's wrong?"

He shrugged. "I'm soaked."

"So am I. Big deal. Look on the bright side, we discovered another clue."

Morris didn't say anything; he just kept walking. Suddenly, he seemed more interested in our surroundings than normal. I don't know why. They were just dark and creepy. He looked up at the sky, then the ground. I heard him mutter something about death; then I got it. His pet.

"Sorry about your fish," I said. "Really."

Morris blinked repeatedly. His cheeks flinched, like he might start to cry. "That pond's been nothing but headaches lately. The rain doesn't help either."

"Is there something I can do?" I asked.

He shook his head. "Nope. It's a James 4:17 thing."

"Huh?"

Morris told me to look it up when I got home. We kept walking. "I may know of someone."

"Someone?" I repeated, wondering why Morris was talking in riddles.

"Someone who can answer questions about the Thorn plantation."

"Who?"

"This guy I know," Morris said, stopping at his street. "He works at a garden store that specializes in pond stuff. He delivered exotic fish to the Thorn family way back when. He must be at least seventy."

"Awesome, Morris." I shook his hand before we split up. "You pulled through again. First you saved my bloody arm from the piranha, now this. You rule."

"No I don't," he said, almost sounding mad. He walked away, still somber. "We'll go tomorrow."

I headed for my house, feeling way too alone. My imagination turned paranoid. A knot on a limb looked like a man's knee. I jumped puddles and jogged, trying to outdistance my thoughts. But I couldn't. So much for jogging; I ran. At my house, I slammed the front door behind me. I expected my dad to ask what kept me, but he didn't. He didn't even chew me out for slamming the front door. He was closed up in his bedroom. I could hear him talking on the phone with someone. I found my sister in her bedroom and asked if it was my mom.

"You catch on quick," she said without looking up from her homework.

I didn't let her wisecrack get to me. We were all feeling edgy without Mom around.

"Good night," I said, turning to leave. It felt

awkward knowing something about Toby that I couldn't share with Sandy—at least, not yet.

"Thanks for making Toby feel welcome tonight," Sandy told me. "He really had a good time."

"Um . . . sure. No problem." I left before she could say anything else. In the hall, I could hear my dad's voice through the bedroom door. He seemed upset over what my mom was telling him. It sounded like he said, "That long, huh?"

I stood there in a funk. My wet clothes gave me the shivers. The thought of my mom being gone even longer didn't help. I walked to my room, not wanting to hear anything else. I changed into dry clothes and carried my silt-smelling jeans to the laundry room. Two more inches and the pile of dirty clothes on the dryer would touch the ceiling. I started to complain, then shut up and ran a load. I sorted out some whites and dumped detergent in the washer. It didn't take long.

Back in my room, I rested on my bed and opened my Bible to James 4:17 to see what Morris was talking about. It read, "Anyone, then, who knows the good he ought to do and doesn't do it, sins."

I reread it a few times trying to figure out what Morris had in mind. What good had he failed to do? Or was the verse for both of us? Maybe he knew we had to purge the piranha from the river, whatever the cost. Was that the good we ought to do? I turned off my light, feeling sorry for myself. Thanks to Morris, I now had one more mystery to solve.

"Tomorrow" turned out to be three days later—our garden store connection was gone for the weekend. We stood in the parking lot as Morris's mom drove away. She was on her way to the gym and would be back in an hour. I stared at the building, wondering how a beat-up old shack could rank as a specialty pond store.

Morris must have read my mind. "Don't worry. You won't be disappointed."

He was right. The inside of the garden store wasn't much to speak of, but out back was incredible, like a jungle of pools and plants.

"Each pond features different fish," Morris explained. He led me to a pond the size of a swimming pool. Plump orange fish with round mouths and white spots slowly flipped their tails. They kissed the surface when they breathed.

I followed the stone path from pond to pond, mesmerized. Some held small fish that swam in schools. Others had turtles.

"Check this one out," Morris said, pointing to a long stretch of water.

"What's in it?"

"Mean fish."

"Like piranha mean?" I asked.

"Close," Morris said. "Gar."

I watched the water, not sure if I wanted to see one or not. Gar had long thin snouts with plenty of teeth. They grew up to six feet long and looked like a cross between a crocodile and a pike.

When Morris asked me to get closer, I hesitated.

"Just don't push me," I said, kneeling beside him at the water's edge.

He didn't.

But someone else did.

Chapter 13

Y ikes!" I gasped. I shoved my hands into the pond to keep from falling in. A tail sliced in my direction. "Ahhh!"

Morris grabbed my collar and pulled me back.

"Are you all right?" an elderly man asked. He had a wiry neck and black-framed glasses. He held a bag of planting soil under each arm. The stench of manure was so thick, you could practically see it. His veins bulged beneath his blotchy skin.

"Um . . . yeah," I said. I dried my hands on my shorts and kept an eye on the pond. A four-foot gar with dagger teeth waited where my hands had been.

"Sorry about that. Let me finish this, then I'll be right with you boys." He hurried down the path and into the store.

"That's our guy," Morris said. "Dirk. He told me he'd help us in any way he could."

The gar cruised away, then circled back around. It watched me.

I put my hands under my armpits, as far from the water as I could get them. "When I grow up, I'm moving to the desert."

Dirk was brushing at his plaid shirt when he returned. He greeted Morris, then introduced himself to me. "Now what can I tell you boys about the Thorn plantation?"

"Everything," I said.

"That could take a while." Dirk found a stool to sit on. "I started delivering fish to their pond when I was twelve years old. That was sixty years ago. Back then the plantation was a sight to behold, beautiful as can be. Then times got hard. The Thorns felt it like everyone else. The family decided to leave the country to start another plantation. Only Elmer Thorn refused to go."

"He stayed back alone?" I questioned.

Dirk nodded. "His wife Myrtle had already died. His grown children moved with the rest of the clan. They came back to visit, but not much— and that was fine with me. One of Elmer's grandkids was about my age and mean as all get out. He used to torment the fish I delivered—and me."

"When did the place start to fall apart?" Morris asked.

"As the years passed, Elmer's money ran out. Eventually, he fell behind on his taxes. The government seized a big piece of the family land and turned it into a park. Elmer always felt wronged. I'm sure the family did too, but they had been out of the country at least twenty years by then. After Elmer died, a groundskeeper looked after the buildings, but not for long. One day he just disappeared."

I thought of what happened to my mom, but didn't bring it up. My interest was in the Thorn heirs who felt wronged, especially the mean grandson who would now be Dirk's age. I asked about him.

"He was a big kid, I remember that."

"You said the Thorn family moved out of the country," I went on. "Do you know where?"

Dirk worked his tongue around his mouth and rubbed his wrinkled face. "Sure do."

"Where?" I asked.

Dirk glanced at one of the ponds. "Brazil. They got themselves a plantation on the Amazon River."

Morris and I loaded the drift net into the rowboat. Dirk's words had confirmed my worst fears. The Amazon and piranha went together like barbs on hooks. In my mind it was settled; Elmer Thorn's grandson had returned and brought his man-eating fish with him. It was all about revenge for land lost a generation ago.

In the two days since meeting with Dirk, Morris had received permission for us to drift downriver in his uncle's rowboat. His mom would meet us on the other side of town with a trailer. Morris's uncle had a dock about a mile upstream of the Thorn plantation, on our side of the river. We borrowed a drift net from Dirk. In return, we promised him a newsworthy specimen. We stopped short of telling him what that might mean. Fortunately, he didn't ask.

"Revenge," I muttered. "That's why the Thorn grandson came back. Revenge. And he brought a thousand piranha with him."

"No way," Morris said. "Not that many."

"How do you know?"

"He couldn't have. They would have caught him at customs."

"So five hundred then. It doesn't matter. Once they start breeding . . ." Thinking about it made me sick. They'd devour more than a rib or rabbit before they were through.

Morris shoved off, then climbed to the stern. I sat in the middle of the wood boat with each hand on an oar. Our plan was to row to the other side of the river, then drop the net. If the piranha were schooling near the Thorn plantation, the net would catch them as we drifted by.

Morris rested his elbows on his knees and stared at the plank bottom of the boat. His eyes were soft. I could tell he was scared, and I didn't blame him. So was I.

I tried to psych him up. "Hey, Morris, I looked up that verse from James."

"Yeah?"

"Yeah. Whoever knows the right thing to do and doesn't do it sins. That's why we're here, right? We're doing the right thing. Saving lives. That's the point, isn't it?"

"Something like that," he said. He scraped the peeling paint with his fingernail. A red chip came loose.

"Then what's wrong?" I asked.

"Nothing," he said. "As long as this boat floats. Nothing."

I leaned into the oars and stroked the water. The clouds blocked the sun and the sky threatened rain. We had jackets and hoods along just in case. The current carried us south, closer to the Thorn plantation.

A woodstork, with its bald gray head and broad white wings, glided upriver hunting for fish. "Do yourself a favor," Morris muttered. "Keep going."

That got to me. Suddenly the boat seemed small. Tiny. What if the net caught a school of piranha? Would it capsize? Would the piranha go ballistic at the sight of our skin? I told myself not to think about it. But I still did.

"This looks good," Morris said. He lowered the net over the side. "Remember, anything other than piranha we release unharmed."

"Check." I pulled a couple more times on the oars until we were fifty feet from the shore. I turned the bow downriver and kept going. Our plan was to row the boat slightly faster than the current. That way the net would fan out like a parachute and catch anything in its path.

Morris checked the knots to make sure the net was secure. He seemed satisfied and offered to switch with me. I moved to the stern just as the Thorn plantation came into view.

"This is it," I said. My arms felt pumped with blood from all the rowing, my skin tight and sweaty. I pulled on the net to check for resistance. If it was full of fish, I would feel their tugs.

"Anything?" Morris asked.

"Not yet."

We passed the tree-lined drive that led to the Thorn plantation. Next came the barn, then stables. Morris kept us moving, past the pond, past the square shacks built for the hired hands. We came to the crumbling white mansion with its boarded-up windows and overgrown porch. Dark and scary. Not a soul was in sight. If Mr. Thorn was there, he was hiding somewhere inside.

"Watch out for the point," I told Morris.

"Got it." He swung the bow toward deeper water.

Our plan was to sweep around the point, then turn into the cove. The net would pull past the boathouse, then around the bank. We'd stay close to the shore along the Thorn property and the park. That's where we had found the bones. That's where the piranha had devoured the rib.

"Are you sure this is deep enough?" I asked. The rocky bulwark that shot out from the point seemed too close for comfort. The river bulged over a submerged boulder just ten feet away.

"The water level's way up," Morris said. "We couldn't hit a rock if we—"

Crunch!

The boat slammed against a solid mass. The wood side fractured like a bone. The sudden jolt sent me to the floor. Morris went over backwards. Water poured between the cracked boards and began to fill the boat.

I grabbed a life vest and handed it to Morris. He put it on. I did the same with another. "Use the bucket!" I stammered. Morris started bailing. He

stepped on the cracked boards to slow the flow.
That helped, but not much. I grabbed the oars
and swung the boat into the cove. I set my sight
on the boathouse dock. If we could make it there
we'd be OK. I pulled at the oars.

Morris bailed water.

It looked good.

Then we stopped. The net snagged on a submerged rock. Water poured in the bow.

"Cut the net," I said. The boat swung with the
current, away from the boathouse and dock.

"It's not my net!" Morris shouted. "I can't."

"You want to sink the boat? Cut it!"

Morris grabbed a knife and hacked loose one
end of the net. It zipped away from the boat and
disappeared in the water. The boat took off again,
but the dock was upriver. Unreachable. Morris
went back to bailing. I rowed hard for the shore.
But it didn't help. We rushed downriver. Then up.
Then down again. I realized what was happening.
We were in the center of the cove. The whirlpool.
And sinking.

Chapter 14

I can't keep up with it," Morris cried. He jammed the bucket into the floor of the boat and scooped up water.

"Faster! Don't give up." I pulled at the oars. My hands burned with blisters. I prayed and fought the current. We made progress. Barely. Water sloshed over the edge. The floor of the boat disappeared. Morris bailed like a madman, flinging water in every direction.

Then I saw it. A frenzy of ripples coming toward us. A school of fish on the move. Fins flashed. I kept going. We broke from the center of the whirlpool. We reached the southern end of the cove. Near the shore. I rowed. Morris bailed.

We passed a cluster of submerged trees.

"Keep going!" Morris shouted.

The school of fish followed us.

Twenty feet to shore. Ten.

Morris dropped the bucket and jumped into the river. He sunk up to his chest.

"What are you doing?" I screamed.

He didn't answer. He grabbed the bowline and heaved. I rowed to help him. Water flowed over the stern. The school of fish bore down. The surface chopped.

Morris strained into the rope until he was waist deep. I grabbed an oar and moved to the back of the boat. I whacked the water for all I was worth. The fish kept coming. Morris pulled. I swung away. Water sprayed.

"Get out!" Morris shouted. He had pulled the boat to a patch of earth between two trees. That was good enough for me. I jumped from the boat just as it filled completely. The feeding frenzy moved in for the kill. I grabbed a tree branch and lifted myself into the air. But not by much. My back hung six inches above the water. I didn't know if piranha could jump, but I wasn't about to find out. I climbed into the tree like an ape.

"Take it easy," Morris said. "They're gone."

I studied the river. Ripples and current but no frenzy.

My heart thumped in high gear. "Where'd they go?"

He shrugged. "Disappeared. Probably just some white bass chasing minnows. They feed in schools."

"I don't think so," I said, panting. "No way. You saw them attack. They wanted us."

We watched and waited. If the fish were there, they didn't want us to know it. Morris returned his attention to the boat. He pulled on the bow to drag it further up the bank. I climbed from the tree and helped him. We were able to get it most of the way out of the water. Morris secured it to a giant willow tree ten feet from the river. We retrieved the net next, still tied to the stern. A section of mesh was torn.

"I don't believe this," Morris said dismally.

I told him I was sorry, but at least we were alive. We spent a while talking over what we should do. Morris's mom wasn't due home for another hour. We could call my dad, but we didn't own a trailer, so it wouldn't do much good. We decided that our best bet was to wait for Morris's mom, especially since the boat belonged to her brother.

That gave us time. I glanced in the direction of the Thorn plantation. All I could think about was evidence, the one thing we needed, the one thing we didn't have. I asked Morris if he wanted to snoop around on foot.

He couldn't believe me. "Haven't you had enough of that place? Besides, you're not allowed to go back there."

"What else are we going to do?" I asked. "Sit here and stare at the boat. Either way it's going to cost us."

"*Us?* You mean, me."

"No way. Whatever it costs to fix the boat, we split it. We're in this together."

Morris avoided looking at me. "You're the best, Nick."

"Come on," I said, standing up. "Something good should come out of this day."

Morris reluctantly agreed and glanced at his watch. "One hour."

"You got it," I said. We made sure the boat was secure, then worked our way through the dense trees and bushes toward the Thorn plantation.

When we got there, we sprinted to a tree in the center of the overgrown yard. I hadn't forgotten what happened on our last visit, the angry moan and heavy footsteps. I held my breath and listened. Nothing.

We agreed to check the boathouse first. Pylons and beams suspended it above the river on the north end of the cove. If Mr. Thorn did have piranha, keeping them there made the most sense. He could release them through the floor of the boathouse. No one would see him. No one would know.

I took off running fast and low, going from tree to tree. Morris followed. Ten feet from the boathouse we paused behind a giant maple. We listened for signs that Mr. Thorn was working inside. Dead silence. Moss covered the walls, along with patches of white paint. Boards warped under the nails. Vines hung from the eaves. The front porch was the only part of the boathouse that didn't have water running beneath it. ·

I pointed to the front window. "Ready?"

Morris nodded. "You first."

I swallowed, said a short prayer, then doubled over and ran. I stepped lightly on the deck. It creaked anyway. Loud. I scurried to the window and pressed myself flat against the wall. I dreaded what would happen if Mr. Thorn found me. Morris watched me from the tree. I waited for steps inside. They never came.

I gave Morris the nod, then raised my head and peered through the glass.

Evidence.

Chapter 15

"T-t-t—" I stuttered.

"Huh?" Morris whispered, in no hurry to join me.

"Tanks! In there!" I waved him over.

Morris hurried to the window. Minnows darted back and forth in one of the aquariums. A hefty catfish swam in another. A third tank had a solitary fish that sent a shiver down my spine. The details matched—silver on the sides, blunt nose, compressed body, protruding lower jaw, too many teeth.

Piranha.

"Evidence," I said. "We finally got it. That's a piranha."

Morris touched the window with his nose. "Are you sure?"

"Definitely," I told him, even though I wasn't. The cloudy sky did a poor job of lighting the room. What's worse, the piranha was in the aquarium against the far wall.

"That could be a white bass," Morris said. "Or even a crappie."

I didn't argue. Three giant plastic drums by the side wall had captured my attention. They looked big enough to hold two hundred gallons each—easy. Latches secured the tops. A long serial number identified each one.

"He must have brought the piranha in those tanks," I said, checking out the rest of the room. Rubber boots, chest-high waders, and fishing poles were on the floor. A map of the river and our town had been tacked to a corkboard. A tower of white buckets leaned in the corner. Test tubes, a microscope, and other scientific-looking stuff covered a table in the center of the room.

"What do you think that stuff's for?" Morris asked.

"He probably created some mutant piranha and brought them here to get revenge." I moved over to the door. "One way to find out." My hand shook as I reached for the knob. The cool brass chilled my palm.

I gave it a turn. Locked. It wouldn't budge. I suggested that we try the big doors at the top of the boat ramp. We crept along the deck that ran the length of the boathouse. Each step took us further over the river. The gray boards looked too worn to support our weight. But we kept going. At the corner I poked my head around. Good thing I did. Old man Thorn glided toward the boathouse in a rowboat. He leaned into the oars with his back to us. He was twenty feet from the end of the dock.

I pushed Morris away in a panic. He clued in and started to run. The boards creaked under our feet. We jumped from the side deck to the weed-covered lawn.

"This way," I said. If we went back the way we had come, Mr. Thorn might see us. We had to keep the boathouse between him and us. That left us one option. Not upriver. Not downriver. But toward the mansion.

We sprinted over the wet mush for the back door. We could see it cracked open. If we tried to go around the building, Mr. Thorn might see us. We crossed the porch and squeezed inside. Dust and dirt covered everything. Musty air filled my nostrils. Rat droppings littered the floor.

I peeked through the opening we had come through. "I don't believe it."

"What?" Morris asked.

"He's coming this way." I searched around as best I could. The boarded-up windows made it hard to see. "Quick. The front door."

We tried it. Locked and bolted. We only had once choice. Hide. We felt our way into the living room and found a closet under the spiral staircase. The back door slammed open. Heavy boots thundered across the kitchen floor. Morris and I squeezed into a wedge of space at the far end of the closet. Total darkness. A spider web tickled my ear. A nail poked my leg. The boots clomped in our direction. Louder. Closer. Then they stopped. He had to be listening for us. I held my breath. He came into the living room. Toward the closet. The doorknob squeaked.

I froze. So did Morris.

"Grandpa?" a voice called out from the kitchen.

"In here," Mr. Thorn grunted. He released the doorknob and stepped back.

Steps came from the kitchen. "Everything all right?"

I recognized the voice. It was Toby's.

Mr. Thorn said he thought he had heard something and came to have a look. I expected him to try the closet, but he didn't. Before long he was reminiscing. "Coming back here makes me think of all kinds of things."

"Is it hard on you?" Toby asked.

"Of course it's hard. You know what they did," Thorn grumbled. "But at least now I have a way to deal with it."

"The sooner the better," Toby said. "It's getting hard keeping things a secret."

"That's for sure. I thought I heard steps at the boathouse."

"No one saw inside, did they?" Toby asked.

"Better not have," Mr. Thorn growled. "But just in case, let's keep looking." The closet door flew open. I turned to stone. I didn't blink or breathe. Silent. Still. The door closed again. God either blinded Mr. Thorn's eyes or made us invisible. Either way, we were safe . . . for now.

I exhaled with relief.

But not for long. Something crawled on my hand. It felt too heavy to be a spider, more like a cockroach. I restrained my first instinct, to squeal and pound it to mush. It crawled up my arm. I tried to shake it loose. The roach scurried higher. For my armpit.

I wanted to jump and run and twitch all at the same time. But I couldn't move.

The voices retreated. "Saturday, Toby—the day we've been waiting for."

The roach climbed higher. Higher. To the edge of my shirt. The voices grew louder again. Heated. And they were coming our way.

Chapter 16

I think I heard something upstairs," Toby said.

"Careful up there," his grandpa warned.

They took the stairs directly above us. The decaying boards moaned like they would break. I shook loose the cockroach and covered my head, certain Grandpa Thorn would come crashing through. At the top of the stairs they moved from one room to the next. We could hear them talking but couldn't understand the words.

We held our position in the closet and waited. Trying to get out ahead of them was too risky. They might see us. Or worse still, catch us.

So we waited.

They finally came back down and left through the back door. We silently slipped from the closet and looked for another way out. Nothing. We had to leave the way we came in.

We cut through the kitchen and I peered out the back door.

"See them?" Morris asked.

I shook my head. On the count of three we bolted across the yard and into the dense foliage that led to the boat. It was where we had left it. From there we crawled and climbed and splashed through the flooded jungle to the park. Morris used the pay phone at the parking lot to call his mom. I kept a watch out for Toby. After making sure we were OK, Morris's mom gave him an earful.

"I'm dead," Morris said as soon as he hung up. He was to walk home while his mom called his uncle.

I told Morris my mom would have reacted the same way . . . if she were home.

If.

"At least your mom's here to get mad."

Morris didn't say anything.

We walked along, both of us feeling down.

"Saturday's only three days away," I said.

"Three days until what?" Morris asked, voicing his frustration. "If they're really going to release hundreds of piranha on Saturday, why did they release some already?"

"Lots of reasons," I argued. "To see how they adapt. To watch their eating habits. Maybe they let out the mature fish to establish a territory for the rest of the school."

Morris seemed to go for that. "They couldn't have released too many, or more people would have noticed."

"Maybe we should tell the police," I suggested. "We saw the piranha in the boathouse."

"The police wouldn't believe us," Morris said dismally. "Not without evidence."

I threw up my hands. "There's that word again. If only we could have nabbed that piranha and brought it with us. *That* would have been evidence."

We kept walking, mulling things over, trying to figure out our next move.

Just before the bridge, I spotted what looked like a dog's skeleton. "Is that what I think it is?" I asked. It had a long nose, sharp teeth, and four legs. There wasn't an ounce of flesh on it.

"Not again," Morris sighed.

I swallowed hard. "Forget about evidence. That could have been us."

The following night I sat in my room looking at my fingers. I held my hand over a lightbulb to see the bones inside. I pictured what my hand would look like with all the flesh torn away. Not pretty.

My mom was on the phone with my dad again. I took that to be a good sign. She missed us so much, she couldn't let her head hit the pillow without hearing our voices. She'd be back soon. This weekend. I hoped after seeing us she'd be unable to leave again. She'd quit her job and we'd learn to get by on less. No problem. I'd take my mom over money any day.

I tightened my hand into a fist and looked out the window. I couldn't see much—just the night. A storm was predicted for tomorrow. A big one. Five inches of rain, maybe more. People with homes on the river had been filling sandbags all day.

I didn't tell my dad about what we saw at the plantation. I knew what he would say. It just *looked* like a piranha. Our theory was too far-fetched. If Mr. Thorn wanted to return to his plantation, he had a right to. If Toby was his grandson, then he should tell Sandy, not you. My dad would want evidence, the one thing we didn't have.

"Nick," my dad called from the hall. "Your mom wants to talk to you."

He was in my room before I could get up. He handed me the white cordless phone.

"Hi, Mom," I said.

My mom told me she missed me and asked how I was.

"OK, I guess. The piranha haven't eaten me yet."

"That's nice," she said with a laugh. "What's it like to play chef?"

"Ask Sandy," I said, frustrated that my mom didn't react to my piranha comment.

For some reason, my dad stayed in my room. As my mom continued to talk, he paced back and forth. He picked up my dirty clothes and straightened the stack of books on my dresser. My mom sounded just as suspicious. It wasn't what she said, but what she didn't. I finally asked her if everything was all right.

"Well, sure," she replied. "Super. The people I work with are great, and they love my work."

"We do too," I said. I wanted to tell her more, but my mouth had trouble translating my heart. I finally blurted out, "I miss you, Mom." I think that got to her because for a while she didn't say anything.

She sniffed, but didn't talk. When she finally did, it was typical mom stuff. "Take care of yourself." "Remember to do your homework." "Listen to your father."

I promised I would, then we said good-bye. Before I handed the phone to my dad, I said, "See you this weekend." I listened for my mom's response, but there wasn't one. My dad grabbed the cordless phone and left for his room.

I sat on my bed, trying to figure out why my mom didn't say anything back. I was still figuring when my dad called me into his room. Sandy was already there sitting in the rocker. I fell across the bed and put my head under a pillow. I knew what was coming.

"I'm afraid I have some bad news," my dad started off. His shoulders dropped with a long sad breath. "Your mom's not coming home."

Chapter 17

"hat do you mean?" Sandy asked.
My dad squeezed his neck. "She can't
make it."

I smacked a pillow to give it some shape. "Why not?"

"They're so impressed with your mom's work, they keep giving her more." My dad bent over and gave my sister a hug.

"So next weekend then?" I suggested.

"Hopefully," my dad said with a shrug.

My sister pointed out that even if Mom didn't make it then, she'd be home the weekend after that—for good.

"That was the plan," my dad said, showing no signs of cheer.

I stopped working the pillow and held still. "What do you mean, *was?*"

My dad's forehead wrinkled. I could practically see the wheels turning as he tried to figure out how to say it. "They've offered your mother an extended position."

I didn't blink or swallow. "Huh?"

My dad explained what *extended* meant. Six to nine months. My mom would leave early Monday morning for the city. She'd stay there until Thursday afternoon, work ten-hour days. She'd have Friday through Sunday off. "That's more nights home than away," my dad told us, just in case we didn't get it.

We got it.

"That stinks," I said.

"Totally," my sister added.

My dad let us vent. He offered sympathy but didn't take our side. He stood up for my mom. He didn't want her to take the position any more than we did, but he understood her dilemma and our financial needs as a family. They'd work through the decision together and trust God to make it clear. "Just keep praying."

We talked until my dad started yawning. I didn't blame him for being tired. When he wasn't working at the factory, he was working around here. But he never complained. He followed through on the Bible verse Sandy read the night before my mom left.

I was glad I didn't tell him about what was happening at the Thorn plantation. My dad had enough on his mind. He was on the verge of becoming a single dad for half of every week, half of every week without his best friend. He and Mom loved being together. They talked about everything, laughed at corny stuff. They still dated once a month and prayed together at night.

What did he care about some stupid piranha?

Now I had another reason to figure out what Grandpa Thorn was planning for Saturday. If we foiled his plans to release a thousand piranha, it would make the evening news. Mom would come back to make sure I was OK and tell me how proud she was.

Then maybe she'd stay.

I stood on the bank of the river holding a fishing pole and net. Morris stood beside me. He held a plastic five-gallon bucket, filled partially with raw meat. Bloated clouds threatened to rain.

Friday had come.

This was our last chance. I had waders on that rose to my knees and kept me dry, not that they would do much good if a school of piranha attacked. The river rushed around my ankles, stronger than usual. I wouldn't venture out far. Shin deep, max. Steel leader, the kind they used for sharks, attached the hook to my line. I passed the line through a bobber to keep the meat from snagging on the bottom.

"Bait me," I told Morris.

He handed me a piece of greasy stew meat. As I pierced it with the hook, blood dripped down my fingers. "I can't believe I'm fishing with raw meat."

"I can't believe I'm fishing, period," Morris added. He curled his lips as I pushed the meat on the hook.

"Here goes nothing." I cast upstream. The stew meat disappeared with a splash. The bobber drifted with the current. It floated past us, quicker than I would have expected.

"Good thing *we're* not out there," Morris said.

When nothing bit, I reeled in and recast. This time I flung the bait and bobber further up-river. I repeated the process several more times without a strike.

"Maybe I should try new bait," I suggested. Morris lifted the bucket and I picked out a stringy piece of beef. It wanted to squirm from my fingers as I pushed it on the hook's sharp point. I dipped the stew piece in the bucket to soak up more blood. "Makes your mouth water, don't it?"

Morris didn't think that was very funny.

I cast as far north as I could, but kept the bait closer to shore. It splashed next to some reeds, then sank. The white and red bobber floated with the current. Then vanished.

"Where'd it go?" Morris asked.

I gave the line a jerk. Something jerked back.

"I got one," I said. I leaned back on the fishing pole and reeled in. The fish darted across the current. The line sliced through the ripples. The fish turned and cut upstream. I waited for it to jump, to get a glimpse. But it stayed below the surface, hidden by the tan water. I turned the crank. The fish snapped and jerked and ran with the line. My reel sang.

"Piranha!" I exclaimed. "It has to be!"

Morris put down the bucket and held the net with both hands. "I'm ready."

I raised the pole and turned the crank, bringing in more line. The fish cut back and forth in an arc. With each turn of the reel, it cut closer.

"Almost there," I said. I watched where the line disappeared beneath the surface. A shape flashed ten feet away. Silver. Round. Compact body. Fierce mouth.

I stepped from the water and pulled the fish into the net. Morris lifted and brought it to shore. My hands tingled. No more wondering or waiting. There it was. Twelve inches of muscle and bone. Gray sides. Angry eyes. Blunt head. Triangle-shaped teeth, razor sharp. Piranha.

I knelt beside it, but not too close. I couldn't shake the feeling that it would flip into the air and latch onto my throat.

"I don't believe it," I sputtered. "It's really a piranha. Here! In our river. A piranha." I looked up at Morris. "This is real! I'm not crazy. I'm not losing it. It's real!"

"I know," Morris said, content to stand.

Using the aluminum rim of the net, I pinned down the piranha so I could remove the hook. A pair of needle-nose pliers did the trick. "Quick, fill the bucket with water."

Morris threw aside the pieces of meat then lowered the bucket into the river. He brought it back full. With the piranha still in the net, I dropped it in the bucket. It flipped its tail, splashing water all over. I watched in awe. It looked just like the pictures. Notch in the forehead. Protruding lower jaw. Teeth and muscle and bone. "Evidence, Morris! We got it! Now we can go to the police."

"No, we can't."

"What do you mean?" I asked, looking up.

Morris stood a few feet away from me with a fillet knife in his hand. "They're mine."

"Huh?"

"The piranha." Morris stepped toward me still clutching the knife. "They're my pets."

Chapter 18

I stepped back. My boot sank in the mud. Water flowed around my ankle.

Morris hovered over the bucket. He looked at the fillet knife in his hand, then back at the piranha. "I got them from a guy I met at the pond store. He lied to me about what they really were. When I put them in my pond, you can guess what they did to the other fish. By the time I got them out, it was too late."

I asked Morris about the fish I found him kneeling beside.

"Her name was Calli. She was my favorite. The piranha injured her, but I didn't think it was that bad. She hung on for two weeks after I got rid of them. She died just before you came over." Morris bent over the bucket, like he wanted to go after the piranha with the knife. "I should have killed them, but I couldn't do it. So instead, I let them go."

"How could you? You saw what they did."

Morris explained his reasoning. He didn't think the piranha would survive the winter. With the swimming season over, what harm could five piranha do?

I shook my head, dumbfounded. "Listen, Morris, I don't want to get you in trouble, but we have to tell the police, or the game warden, or someone. You saw the bones. The skeletons. What if—"

"Not yet," Morris said. "Not until we know the truth."

"We know the truth."

"No, we don't!" Morris protested. He held up his fingers. "I let five fish go so they could die free. Five. Got it? Not enough to eat a dog or a deer. I've done my research. It would take a school of piranha. Not five."

I thought about what Morris said. It made sense. "Who sold you the piranha?"

"I don't know. Some guy I met in the pond store parking lot. He said he couldn't keep the fish and would have to kill them. He just gave them to me."

I couldn't figure out why Mr. Thorn would leak out some piranha ahead of time.

Neither could Morris. "Maybe that guy and Thorn aren't even connected."

"Or maybe he wanted to spread the piranha around," I said. "Shift the blame."

Morris searched upriver toward the plantation. "Something's going on up there."

I watched the piranha circle in the bucket. The verse Morris quoted now made sense. Not doing the right thing had burdened him with guilt so that he was edgy and somber. No wonder he had a love/hate attitude toward the river. He wanted to know what had happened to his pets, but at the same time, never wanted to see them again.

"Forgive me?" Morris asked, extending his hand.

I shook it and told him I did. We'd try and catch the other four, then move on to phase two: the boathouse.

We didn't catch the other four. Or even get a nibble.

The sun slipped behind the trees. Dusk settled over the water. A blue heron lifted from the reeds and flapped for cover.

"Ready?" I asked.

Morris nodded. He hid the bucket in a thicket a short way from the water. We left the subject of what we would do with the piranha alone. I didn't want to get into it again. Morris had freaked me out enough already. I felt bad for him, but that wouldn't keep me from turning in the piranha to the authorities. They had to know. If the other piranha weren't captured and they reproduced, the native fish and wildlife might be wiped out, not to mention the people who swam in the river.

I worked that thought over in my mind as we headed for the Thorn plantation. Was that their plan? If it was, my dad couldn't get mad at me for this. I wasn't going where I didn't belong; I was trying to save our town.

At the end of the park, the narrow trail we had taken before was under too much water. We had to climb the fence. My boots slipped on the chain-link, but I finally got over. As I came down on the other side, the clouds burst. Rain poured down, cooling my hair and soaking my shirt.

"Stay low," I said. We hunkered down and scratched our way through the thick bushes and trees. The river had flooded new areas, forcing us to wade. Grass floated with the current, along with rust-colored leaves, hiding anything and everything beneath the surface.

I thought about Toby and hoped he had picked a long movie for his date with Sandy. I prayed that Mr. Thorn had taken the night off too. But that wasn't essential. We had a plan.

We crawled and splashed toward Whirlpool Cove. I picked my steps carefully. So far so good. No piranha or bones.

"What was that?" Morris asked.

"Not again," I muttered.

Again.

Morris lifted a thick bone the size of a club. It had to be from either a horse or cow.

"See what I mean?" Morris said. "Five piranha, huh? No way."

He was right. And if the piranha did that to a cow, what would they do to us?

I kept going until something nicked my boot and took a piece of rubber with it. Water seeped in and soaked my sock. But I couldn't stop. I pushed aside vines and branches. I splashed through the river and rain until the boathouse came into view. The glow of a dim light filled the side window. So much for Grandpa Thorn taking the night off. Good thing we had a plan. We silently rounded the cove to the tree closest to the boathouse.

"You're sure he will come after me?" Morris asked.

"Yep. You watch."

Our plan was for Morris to make a loud noise and draw Mr. Thorn up to the mansion. While Morris hid and Mr. Thorn searched for him, I would nab some evidence from the boathouse and get out. We'd go to the police, game warden, or both.

The door to the boathouse was closed and the windows were shut tight. Rain pelted the river and leaves and filled the air with sound.

"Make it loud," I said.

Morris sprang from the tree and sprinted for the back porch. He was halfway there when a bloody scream erupted from the old mansion. He froze in the middle of the yard. The rain showered him. He watched me in confused panic. So much for our plan.

The voice belonged to a woman. It sounded familiar.

My actions told Morris what to do. I ran for the mansion to help whoever was screaming. Morris followed. We crossed the back porch and hurried inside.

"It sounded like it came from upstairs," I whispered.

We quietly took the decaying stairs two at a time. Morris held the fillet knife in front of him. We were at the top when a shout came from below. "Hey! Where do you think you're going?"

We bolted down the hallway into a bedroom.

Heavy boots pounded the stairs. We listened for the woman. Nothing.

The aged voice shouted again. "Come back here!"

We closed the bedroom door and tried to lock it. It wouldn't. We checked our options. The room was empty, no chair or furniture to barricade the door.

"The closet," Morris said. He made it there.

I didn't. My foot crashed through the rotten boards.

I yanked wildly.

But the floor wouldn't let go.

Chapter 19

orris disappeared into the closet. Boots clomped to the top of the stairs. They echoed in the hall. Splintered wood jabbed my ankle, holding it.

"Come on," Morris urged. He stood in the closet and pointed at the ceiling. "There's an attic."

"Hide," I whispered. I yanked at my foot. A nail ripped the heel of my rubber boot.

The doorknob turned. Slowly. I watched it, terrified. My adrenaline surged, but I couldn't get free. I mumbled a frantic prayer for God's help.

Morris rushed to my side.

"What are you doing?" I asked him. "Hide!"

"No chance," he told me. He pried at the rotten planks.

I watched the doorknob. It turned all the way.

Then the woman screamed again. The door-knob released and the boots tromped down the hall, down the stairs. We heard the front door slam.

Morris grabbed my arm and lifted. I worked at the boot until it pulled free, but not before the nail cut my skin. We crossed the hall and entered another room. My white sock turned red. But I didn't care. We went straight to the window.

Mr. Thorn disappeared into the boathouse. The door swung shut.

"Did you see the woman?" Morris gasped.

"No, but he must have her."

"Either that or she's still in here," Morris said.

We looked around the room, queasy at the thought of a woman being trapped somewhere in the rotting mansion. We had to check. I went one way down the hall. Morris went the other. Boards creaked. I stepped lightly. Wallpaper hung in curled fragments. Spider webs draped from the ceiling lamps.

"Anyone in here?" I asked softly.

No one answered.

Rain lashed at the house. The smell of mildew and decay filled the air.

"Hello?" Morris called out. "We're here to help."

A board snapped under my foot. I shifted my weight before it could break.

I pushed open the bathroom door. Nothing. I checked the closet. Empty.

I went from room to room until I met Morris at the top of the stairs. We hurried down and repeated the process on the bottom floor. No use. We struck out.

I checked my cut foot. The bleeding had nearly stopped. "Mr. Thorn must have her."

Morris nodded gravely. "The boathouse."

We went to a window on the side of the house that wasn't visible from the boathouse. We pushed and pried the plywood until we could squeeze out. We dropped to the ground, and from there we made a wide circuit through a grove of trees. We worked toward the boathouse, keeping well out of sight. We returned to the thick overgrowth on the bank of the river. The boathouse was just twenty feet away.

"Remember," I said. "If I don't come back, you go for help."

"You'll come back," Morris said.

I snaked through the bushes. My foot ached from the cut. Blood oozed. I thanked God my tetanus shot was current. At the pylons beneath the boathouse, I started to climb. I hung from a wood post and stepped on another. I heard Grandpa Thorn above me. He spoke in short bursts, angry. The woman gasped.

I grabbed the windowsill to look inside. It was damp. Slippery. I clung to the board and pulled myself up. The first thing I noticed was the dissected piranha on the table. Then I saw the woman at the same time she spotted me. She screamed and lifted her hands just as mine came loose.

I fell backward, too stunned to scream back.

The woman was my mom.

I landed in the river with a splash. The current pulled me from shore. The dirty water burned my cut. The bank shrunk away as I drifted to deep water. Suddenly my rubber boots felt like lead weights. I reached down to pull them off, but swallowed a brown mouthful and started to cough.

Of all the places to fall in the river, I picked the worst. The deadliest. Now I knew how my mom felt when the same thing happened to her. I swirled around the cove. Everything worked against me. My clothes. My boots. I thought of the blood on my ankle and the piranha. How long until the frenzy? The jaws and teeth and blood. How long?

I jerked at my boots to free them. I coughed and tried to swim. My hair covered my eyes. The current kept me moving. Something bumped my ankle. Something sharp. I flailed at the water, certain a feeding frenzy would follow.

"Hang on!" Morris shouted. He pointed at the boathouse. The back doors opened. A boat slid down the ramp into the water. Mr. Thorn sat in the stern. He yanked the cord to start the outboard.

The river owned me. I didn't fight it. I couldn't. Another nick against my ankle. "Ouch!" I grimaced. The log came next, out of nowhere. I bumped my head hard. Everything started to spin. Rain pummeled me. The river swallowed me. I took in more water. Coughed. Sharp points jabbed my legs. My feet.

I no longer feared old man Thorn. I just thought about my mom. What would he do to her once he finished with me? The boat split the whirlpool, zooming in my direction. The hull would split my skull.

Morris jumped and shouted on the bank.

My eyes went blurry. Fins broke the surface. Teeth. I thought I heard my mom. The outboard engine. A weathered hand came at me.

More swallowing. Choking. Cutting.

Water filled me and buried me.

Then I was gone.

Chapter 20

I squinted into the bright light. I coughed and rolled to my side. Something hard poked my spine. My head throbbed. I blinked to get my bearings. The rain had stopped. A face blocked the light. I recognized it.

Mom!

"Where am I?" I muttered. My throat burned. My lungs ached. I had a bad taste in my mouth. I rolled my head. The rounded hull of the boat came into focus, then a oar. I arched my back to ease the pain. My mom reached in and pulled the anchor chain from under me.

I recognized another face. Morris.

He stood beside the rowboat.

I savored a deep breath of air. I started to relax.

Then Mr. Thorn stepped from behind me.

I lurched to get away.

"Relax," my mom said. She put a hand on my shoulder and laid me down. "If it hadn't been for Mr. Timber, you wouldn't be here right now."

"Mr. Timber?" I sputtered fragments of everything I was thinking. "But he tried to get us. And you screamed. And the piranha . . ." My words trailed off as I tried to make sense of it all.

My mom offered a soothing smile. "When I heard Toby's last name, I made a few calls. The Department of Parks and Recreation got back to me this morning with the answer I was hoping for. I finished work early and drove here to see him. I had to. Mr. Timber was the groundskeeper here when I was a girl. He saved my life."

"S-saved your life?" I stuttered.

"He sure did," my mom beamed. "And today he saved yours. He got to you just in time."

I nearly gagged. "Him? He was out to get us."

Mr. Timber laughed. "*Get* you? Not me. I just wanted to scare you off. You wouldn't believe how many bad apples come around here. That's why I got your mom out of the old mansion."

"But Mom, you screamed—twice. We heard it."

"Just rats," my mom explained. "Mr. Timber was giving me a tour for old time's sake."

I lay there trying to put the pieces together. Some fit. Others made no sense at all.

"But we heard you say something about

Saturday, that everyone would know. You were mad. You told Toby—"

The door to the boathouse flung open.

"What about Toby?" my sister asked.

"Yeah?" Toby said. "What about me?"

My dad followed them in and came to my side.

"He's fine," my mom said, putting her arms around my dad. She updated everyone on what happened.

"About what you said earlier," Mr. Timber continued. "You've confused two different things. I was mad at myself for the mistake I made years ago. I never should have let your mom play in the trees that day."

"I never should have asked," my mom added.

"Saturday's entirely different," Mr. Timber went on. "It represents a new era for this plantation. As your mom found out, I work for the Department of Parks and Recreation. I've been assigned to conduct a feasibility study."

"A what?" I asked.

"A study to see if it's financially and ecologically feasible to restore the plantation. The land and buildings have been donated to the state by the Thorn family. We'd like to turn it into a park and cultural center."

"Cool," Sandy said. "Will it work?"

Mr. Timber nodded. "If you ask me, it's a go,

especially now that we've solved our piranha problem."

I learned that Mr. Timber had caught the other piranha during one of his environmental impact studies. They were in the large tank against the wall except for one he dissected to run some tests. The piranha swam from one side of the glass to the other, snapping their tails like whips. Even in an aquarium they scared me. Blunt heads, diamond-sharp teeth, dense bodies. All muscle and bone. Deadly.

I climbed from the boat and walked over to them. "I still don't get it. Five piranha aren't enough." I told Mr. Timber about the skeletons we had found.

"Ah, the bones," Mr. Timber said. "Come with me."

We followed him to the rear of the boathouse. He pushed open the big double doors. From the top of the ramp, we scanned the river.

"See over there?" Mr. Timber pointed to the south end of the cove. "That's where the Thorn family used to bury their pets. Normally it's not under water. The river washed the soil away. That explains the bones."

I started to laugh. It was too much to handle. Just five piranha, and the Thorn family had nothing to do with it.

"What happens to me?" Morris asked.

Mr. Timber rubbed his chin. "It'll help if you can describe the guy who gave you the piranha. Either way, I'll have to file a report. You'll probably have to put in some community service hours. If you have the choice, I can use your help around here."

"Just tell me when," Morris said. "I'll be here."

"Me too," my mom added.

We all looked at her.

"You will?" I asked. "How? You won't even be here." I turned and went back to the front of the boathouse.

My mom caught up with me. "Nick, a long time ago I learned what happens when you do something that looks tempting, even though you know you shouldn't. I've spent most of my life afraid of the river because of it." She squeezed my shoulders. "I turned down the job."

I gave my mom a hug and wouldn't let go just in case she changed her mind. Having her gone was a nightmare—a miserable, dreary, bad-food, messy-house nightmare.

My sister took my place as soon as I let go. My dad used the opportunity to pull me aside. He told me that I would also be volunteering time at the plantation as a consequence of disobeying and coming back. I didn't argue. That was fair.

We talked for a little longer in the boathouse about everything that had happened. Toby admitted to being behind the tree near our house but had no idea how the skull got in our trash can.

"I was going to come visit," he said sheepishly. "But I chickened out."

Sandy thought that was cute, of course.

Mr. Timber spoke up next. "Who's ready for a tour of the plantation? I'll give you a sneak preview of tomorrow's press conference."

That sounded great to everyone—except me.

"I think I'll stay here," I said. I showed them my cut foot and said I wanted to rest for a little while and get my bearings.

They tried to talk me into going, but finally left me alone.

That gave me time to pray. I asked God to forgive me for misjudging the Thorn family and trespassing on their property. Instead of wiping out our town with piranha, they were donating a plantation. Incredible. I also thanked the Lord for my mom's decision to stay and that I was still alive to celebrate it. Like her, I had learned a lesson I would never forget: sometimes, doing the right thing means saying no to the wrong thing— no matter how tempting it seems at the time.

The piranha swam back and forth across the front of the aquarium. They watched me with open mouths, powerful jaws, and razor-sharp teeth. They looked as dangerous as ever. Deadly. Suddenly, the aquarium glass seemed a little too thin. Maybe a tour wasn't such a bad idea after all.

I pulled open the door to the boathouse, but didn't get far.

A frigid hand grabbed my neck.

"It's about time," my dad said. He told me he wanted to make sure I was OK.

"I am now," I answered.

We stood on the porch of the boathouse and surveyed the rest of the plantation.

Everyone else had gathered under the gazebo across the lawn. Mr. Timber spoke with expressive hands as he explained all the restoration projects to come. My mom beamed from ear to ear and kept looking back at me and my dad.

"Mom sure is excited about the plans," I said. "Look at her."

"There's more to it than that, Nick," my dad said. He winked at my mom. "She's coming home."

Mr. Timber led the group toward the mansion. My mom slipped and landed with a splat. Rather than get up, she just laughed and lifted her hands toward my dad. He didn't hesitate. He jumped from the porch and ran through the rain to help her.

"She's coming home," I whispered, thankfully. "She's coming home."